Maxims and Reflections

Johann Wolfgang von Goethe

Maxims and Reflections

Copyright © 2022 Indo-European Publishing

The present edition is a reproduction of previous publication of this classic work. Minor typographical errors may have been corrected without note; however, for an authentic reading experience the spelling, punctuation, and capitalization have been retained from the original text.

ISBN: 978-1-64439-697-1

CONTENTS

TRANSLATOR'S PREFACE

I

The translation of Goethe's "Prose Maxims" now offered to the public is the first attempt that has yet been made to present the greater part of these incomparable sayings in English. In the complete collection they are over a thousand in number, and not more perhaps than a hundred and fifty have already found their way into our language, whether as contributions to magazines here and in America, or in volumes of miscellaneous extract from Goethe's writings. Some are at times quoted as though they were common literary property. To say that they are important as a whole would be a feeble tribute to a work eloquent for itself, and beyond the need of praise; but so deep is the wisdom of these maxims, so wide their reach, so compact a product are they of Goethe's wonderful genius, that it is something of a reproach to literature to find the most of them left untranslated for the sixty years they have been before the world. From one point of view, the neglect they have suffered is in no way surprising: they are too high and severe to be popular so soon; and when they meet with a wide acceptance as with other great works, much of it will rest upon authority. But even for the deeper side of his writings, Goethe has not been denied a fair measure of popular success. No other author of the last two centuries holds so high a place, or, as an inevitable consequence, has been attacked by so large an army of editors and commentators; and it might well be supposed by now that no corner of his work, and least of all one of the best, had remained almost unnoticed, and to the majority unknown. Many of these maxims were early translated into French, but with little success; and even in Germany it was only so late as the year 1870 that they

iv

appeared in a separate form, with the addition of some sort of critical comment and a brief explanation of their origin and history.[1]

But although to what is called the reading public these maxims are as yet, no less in fact than in metaphor, a closed book, its pages have long been a source of profit and delight to some of those who are best able to estimate their value. What that value is, I shall presently endeavour to explain. No one, I think, can perceive their worth without also discerning how nearly they touch the needs of our own day, and how greatly they may help us in facing certain problems of life and conduct, some of them, in truth, as old as the world itself, which appear to us now with peculiar force and subtlety.

It was in this respect that they were warmly recommended to me some years ago by my excellent friend, Professor Harnack, the historian of Dogma, a writer with a fine and prudent enthusiasm for all ennobling literature. It is to him that I owe the resolve to perform for the maxims, as far as I could, the office of translator; a humble office, but not, as I have good reason to know, without its difficulty, or, as I venture to hope, without its use. Of many of them the language is hardly lucid even to a German, and I have gratefully to acknowledge the assistance I have received from the privilege of discussing them with so distinguished a man of letters.

To Professor Huxley I am also deeply indebted. I owe him much for friendly encouragement, and still more for help of an altogether invaluable kind; for in its measure of knowledge and skill, it is admittedly beyond the power of any other living Englishman. The maxims deal, not alone with Life and Character, where most of them are admirable, but also with certain aspects of Science and Art; and these are matters in which I could exercise no judgment myself, although I understood that, while many of the maxims on

---

[1] Goethe's Sprüche in Prosa: zum ersten Mal erläutert und auf ihre Quellen zurückgeführt von G. v. Loeper, Berlin, 1870. This forms the text of the translation.

Science and Art were attractive, they were not all of great merit. Professor Huxley not only did me the honour to select the maxims on Science, but he was further good enough to assist me with them, and to read and approve the translation as it now stands. The weight and the interest of his authority will thus give additional value to that section of the book, and also do much to overcome the objections that exist to making a selection at all.

For a selection is a necessary evil. It is an evil because, even if it leaves the best, it takes away something of a man's work; if it shows us the heights he has reached, it obliterates the steps of his ascent; it endangers thoughts that may be important but imperfectly understood; and it hinders a fair and complete judgment. But in the end it is a necessity: we are concerned chiefly with the best and clearest results, and it is only the few who care to follow the elaborate details of effort and progress, often painful and obscure. There is no author with whom, for most readers, selection is so necessary as it is with Goethe; and in no other kind of literature is it so amply justified or so clearly desirable as where the aim is to state broad truths of life and conduct and method in a manner admitting of no mistake or uncertainty. When a writer attempts achievements, as Goethe did, in almost every field of thought, it need be no surprise to any one who has heard of human fallibility that in solid results he is not equally successful everywhere. In deciding what shall be omitted, there is no difficulty with maxims which time has shown to be wrong or defective; they have only an historical interest. But great care is necessary with others that are tentative, questionable, or obscure enough to need the light of a commentary, sometimes dubious; where for most of us there is never much profit and always occasion for stumbling. I count it a singular piece of good fortune that the choice of the scientific maxims should be undertaken by so eminent a judge of their practical value, who is also a scholar in the language and a great admirer of Goethe in his other and better known productions. For if a writer of this immense versatility cannot always hope to touch the highest goal, it is well that all his efforts should be weighed in a later day by the best and friendliest knowledge.

The maxims on Art were at first a matter of some little difficulty. It is plain, I think, that they are below the others in value and interest; and in any collection of sayings the less there is of general worth, the more delicate becomes the task of choosing the best. If I omitted them all, the selection would not be duly representative, and it seemed likely that some at least were worthy of being preserved, if only to illustrate Goethe's theories. I therefore sought the best advice; and here again I have to tender my thanks for assistance second to none in skill and authority,—that of Sir Frederick Leighton, kindly given under circumstances which much increase my obligation. For it is my duty to say that Sir Frederick Leighton had no desire, but rather reluctance, to make a selection from maxims on Art which he was often not prepared to endorse, or to regard as in any way commensurate with Goethe's genius; and nevertheless he did me the honour to point out a few which I might insert, as being of interest partly for their own sake, partly also for the name of their author.

The maxims on Science and Art are, however, when taken together, hardly a fifth of this volume. The others I have selected on the simple and I hope blameless principle of omitting only what is clearly unimportant, antiquated, of past or passing interest, of purely personal reference, or of a nature too abstruse to stand without notes of explanation, which I should be sorry to place at the foot of any of these pages. I have also omitted eleven maxims drawn from Hippocrates On Diet; fifteen containing an appreciation of Sterne, together with some twenty more which Goethe himself translated from a curious work wrongly attributed to that writer. It will be convenient if I state that I have thus omitted some hundred and twenty out of the six hundred and fifty-five which make up the section styled in the original Ethisches, which I translate by Life and Character, the section which also contains the maxims on Literature, now collected and placed in a separate section with those on Art. Sir Frederick Leighton chose thirty-five out of a hundred and eighteen on Art, and Professor Huxley seventy-six out of two hundred and eighty on Science.

Having thus acknowledged but in no way discharged a triple debt of gratitude, it will be next in order if I briefly state the history of the work which now appears in an English dress, before attempting to speak of its nature and value.

The publication of the maxims belongs to the later, that is to say, the last thirty, years of Goethe's life; and the greater number of them appeared only in the last ten, while some are posthumous.

It is impossible to say with certainty at what period he began the observations which were afterwards to come before the world in this shape; nor is the question of any real interest except to pedantic students of such matters. It is probable that, like most writers, Goethe was in the habit of noting transient thoughts of his own, as well as opinions of others that suggested more than they actually conveyed; and of preserving for further use what he had thus, in his own words, written himself and appropriated from elsewhere— Eigenes and Angeeignetes. The maxims grew out of a collection of this character. It was a habit formed probably in early life, for somewhere in the Lehrjahre—a work of eighteen years' duration, but begun at the age of twenty-seven—he makes Wilhelm Meister speak of the value of it. But there are reasons for thinking that most of the maxims, as they now stand, were not alone published but also composed in his last years. The unity of meaning which stamps them with a common aim; the similarity of the calm, dispassionate language in which they are written; the didactic tone that colours them throughout, combine to show that they are among the last and ripest fruits of his genius. Some were certainly composed between the ages of fifty and sixty; more still between that and seventy; while there is evidence, both internal and external, proving that many and perhaps most of them were his final reflections on life and the world. This it is that adds so much to their interest for as he himself finely says in one of the last of them, "in a tranquil mind thoughts rise up at the close of life hitherto unthinkable; like blessed inward voices alighting in glory on the summits of the past."

But whenever all or any of them were written, and whatever revision they may have undergone, none were published until 1809, when Goethe was sixty years of age. It was then that he brought out Die Wahlverwandschaften. A few of the maxims on Life and Character were there inserted as forming two extracts from a journal often quoted in the earlier part of the story. "About this time," writes Goethe, as he introduces the first of these extracts, "outward events are seldomer noted in Ottilie's diary, whilst maxims and sentences on life in general, and drawn from it, become more frequent. But," he adds, "as most of them can hardly be due to her own reflections, it is likely that some one had given her a book or paper, from which she wrote out anything that pleased her." A few more maxims appeared eight years later in Kunst und Alterthum, a magazine founded by Goethe in 1816 and devoted to the discussion of artistic questions; and a larger number first saw the light in the same publication at various dates until its extinction in 1828. Some of the observations on Science had meanwhile been incorporated with two treatises on branches of that subject.

Eckermann tells a curious story of the way in which Goethe then continued the publication of the maxims. Wilhelm Meisters Wanderjahre had appeared in its first form in 1821. Afterwards, in 1829, Goethe decided to remodel and lengthen it, and to make two volumes out of what had originally been only one. His secretary was employed to copy it out in its revised form. He wrote in a large hand, which gave the impression that the story might well fill even three volumes; and directions to this effect were sent to the publisher. But it was soon discovered that the last two volumes would be very thin, and the publisher asked for more manuscript. Goethe, in some perplexity, sent for Eckermann, and producing two large bundles of unpublished papers, containing, as he said, some very important things, — "opinions on life, literature, science and art, all mingled together," proposed to him to lengthen out the volumes by inserting selections from them. "You might," he suggested, "fill the gaps in the Wanderjahre by making up some six or eight sheets from these detached pieces. Strictly speaking, they have nothing to do with the story; but we may justify the proceeding by the fact that I mention an archive in Makarie's house, in which such miscellanies are preserved. In this way we shall not only get over our difficulty, but find a good vehicle for giving much interesting matter to the world." Eckermann approved the plan, and divided his selection into two parts; and when the new edition of the Wanderjahre appeared, one of them was styled Aus Makariens Archiv, and the other Betrachtungen im Sinne der Wanderer: Kunst, Ethisches, Natur. The remainder of the unpublished maxims appeared posthumously, either in the Nachgelassene Werke in 1833, or in the quarto edition of 1836.

Instructions had been given to Eckermann to collect all the maxims, arrange them under different heads, and include them in appropriate volumes; but he resolved to deviate from his instructions to the extent of publishing them all together; and the alteration is certainly an advantage. A slight re-arrangement was made by von Loeper, who was deterred from undertaking a more radical one, although he thought it might be done with profit, by the consideration that when a literary work of undesigned and fortuitous form has lived any number of years in a certain shape, that fact alone is a weighty argument against any change in it. In a translation, perhaps, where the work is presented anew and to a fresh public, the change might be allowable; and I should have undertaken it, had there not been a more serious reason, which von Loeper also urges, against any attempt at systematic re-arrangement: the further fact, namely, that many of the maxims have a mixed character, placing them above our distinctions of scientific and ethical, and making it difficult to decide under which heading they ought to fall. I have, therefore, generally followed the traditional order; with this exception, that, for obvious reasons, the maxims dealing with Literature are here placed together; and as only a few of those on Art appear in these pages, I have included them in the same section. In one or two cases I have united closely connected maxims which are separated in the original; and, for the sake of a short title, I have slightly narrowed the meaning of the word Spruch, which applies to any kind of shrewd saying, whether it be strictly a maxim or an aphorism. Some little liberties of this kind may, I think, be taken by a translator anxious to put the work before his own public in an orderly and convenient form.

The last section in this book requires a word of explanation. It is a little essay on Nature which is to be found with a variety of other fragments in the last volume of Goethe's collected works. Too short to stand by itself, if it appears at all, it must be in company with kindred matter; and as a series of aphorisms, presenting a poetic view of Nature unsurpassed in its union of beauty and insight, it is no inappropriate appendage to the maxims on Science. It is little known, and it deserves to be widely known. I venture to think that even in Germany the ordinary reader is unaware of its existence. For us in England it was, so to speak, discovered by Professor Huxley, who many years ago gave a translation of it as a proem to a scientific periodical. Perhaps that proem may yet be recovered as good salvage from the waters of oblivion, which sooner or later overwhelm all magazines. Meanwhile I put forward this version.

For sixty years this essay has stood unquestioned in Goethe's works; but doubt has recently been cast on its authorship. The account hitherto given rests upon the excellent ground of Goethe's own declaration. The essay, it appears, was written about the year 1780, and offered to the Duchess Amalia. Some time after her death it was found amongst her papers, and sent to Goethe in May, 1828, when, as he wrote to his friend the Chancellor von Müller, he could not remember having composed it; although he recognised the writing as that of a person of whose services he used to avail himself some forty years previously. That at so great a distance of time a prolific author could not recall the composition of so short a piece is not, indeed, improbable; but Goethe proceeded to say that it agreed very well with the pantheistic ideas which occupied him at the age of thirty, and that his insight then might be called a comparative, which was thus forced to express its strife towards an as yet unattained superlative. Notwithstanding this declaration, the essay is now claimed as the production of a certain Swiss friend of Goethe's, by name Tobler, on external evidence which need not be examined here, and on the internal evidence afforded by the style, which is certainly more pointed and antithetic than is usual with Goethe. But a master of language who attempted every kind of composition may well have attempted this; and even those who credit an otherwise unknown person with the actual writing of the essay candidly admit that it is based upon conversations with Goethe. It is so clearly inspired with his genius that he can hardly be forced to yield the credit of it to another.

III

It is no wish or business of mine to introduce these maxims by adding one more to the innumerable essays, some of them admirable, which have been written on Goethe. I have found the translation of one of his works a harder and certainly a more profitable task than a general discourse on them all; and I profoundly believe that, rather than read what has been written on Goethe, it is very much better to read Goethe himself. It is in this belief that I hope the present translation may help in a small way to increase the direct knowledge of him in this country. But there are some remarks which I may be allowed to make on the nature and use of maxims, and the peculiar value of those of Goethe; so far, at least, as they deal with life and character and with literature. If Professor Huxley could be induced to publish the comments which he made to me as I read him the scientific maxims, besides being the best of introductions to that section of the book, they would form a keen and clear review of Goethe's scientific achievements, and an emphatic testimony to his wonderful anticipations of later theories.

Between a maxim, an aphorism, and an apophthegm, and in a more obvious degree, between these and an adage and a proverb, the etymologist and the lexicographer may easily find a distinction. But they are, one and all, fragments of the wisdom of life, treasured up in short, pithy sentences that state or define some general truth of experience; and perhaps with an adage and a maxim, enjoin its practice as a matter of conduct. In the literature of every age there have been writers who, instead of following a less severe method, thus briefly record the lessons taught them by a wide view of the doings of men; from the dim, far-off beginnings of Ptah Hotep the Egyptian to the authors of the Proverbs of Solomon and the Book of Wisdom, from Theognis and Plutarch downwards to our own time. They give us the shrewdest of their thoughts, detached from the facts which gave them birth. But the professed writers of maxims are not the only or always the best authors of them. There is no great writer who is not rich in wise sentences; where we have the advantage of seeing for ourselves the train of thought that induced and the occasion that called them forth. Terse and pregnant sayings are scattered innumerably through the pages of the finest poets, the great orators, philosophers, and historians, wherever they touch the highest level of truth and insight; be it in the lofty interpretation of life, the defence of action or policy, the analysis of character and conduct, or the record of progress; and then it is that large ideas and wide observations take on imperceptibly the nature of maxim or aphorism, illumining, like points of light, whole fields of thought and experience. And the test of their value is that they lose little or nothing by being deprived of their particular context and presented as truths of general import. A collection of proverbs, shrewd sayings, and pointed expressions, taken from the whole range of Greek and Latin literature, was made by the industry of Erasmus in his great folio of Adagia; and perhaps some future student, as diligent as he, may gather up the aphoristic wisdom in the writings of modern times. Goethe himself has in all his great works a wealth of aphorism unsurpassed by any other writer whatever, even though it be Montaigne or Bacon or Shakespeare; and sayings of his not to be found in this collection are some of the best that he uttered.

The besetting sin of the maxim-writer is to exaggerate one side of a matter by neglecting another; to secure point and emphasis of style, by limiting the range of thought; and hence it is that most maxims present but a portion of truth and cannot be received unqualified. They must often be brought back to the test of life itself, and confronted and compared with other sides of the experience they profess to embody. And when a maxim stands this trial and proves its worth, it is not every one to whom it is of value. To some it may be a positive evil. It makes the strongest appeal to those who never see more than one aspect of anything, hardening their hearts and blunting their minds; and even to those who could make a good use of it, there are times when it may mislead and be dangerous. Maxims in their application seem to need something of the physician's art: they must be handled with care, and applied with discretion. Like powerful drugs they may act with beneficent effect on a hardy constitution; they may brace it to effort, or calm the fever of a misguided activity; but great is the mischief they work where the mind is weak or disorganised. As a medicine may save a man at one time that would kill him at another, so the wise counsel of to-day may easily become the poisonous suggestion of to-morrow.

With writers who depend for effect on mere qualities of style and ignore the weightier matters of depth and truth of observation, Goethe has nothing in common; nor with those who vainly imagine that insight is a kind of art, with a method that may be learned and applied. By constant practice a man of literary talent may, it is true, attain a fair mastery of language terse and attractive, and then set himself, if he will, to the deliberate creation of aphoristic wisdom or a philosophy of proverbs; mistaking the dexterous handling of a commonplace for the true process of discovery. The popular literature of the last generation supplies a terrible instance of the length to which the manufacture of maxims can thus be carried, for a time with immense success; and we have seen how a few years suffice to carry them and their author to obscurity. How different is the true process! The maxim that increases knowledge and enriches literature is of slow and rare appearance; it springs from a fine faculty of observation which is in no one's arbitrament, and only less rare than the gift of utterance which adds charm to a thought that itself strikes home with the power of impregnable truth. No amount or intensity of effort will alone produce it; but to the mind of genius it comes like a sudden revelation, flashing its light on a long course of patient attention. "What we call Discovery," says Goethe, "is the serious exercise and activity of an original feeling for truth. It is a synthesis of world and mind, giving the most blessed assurance of the eternal harmony of things."

It is, then, depth and truth and sanity of observation which chiefly mark these sayings of Goethe. It is no concern of his to dazzle the mind by the brilliance of his wit; nor does he labour to say things because they are striking, but only because they are true. He is always in contact with realities, always aiming at truth; and he takes a kindly and a generous view of the world. He has none of the despair that depresses, none of the malice that destroys. There are writers who profess to honour a lofty ideal by a cynical disparagement of everything that falls short of it; who unveil the selfish recesses of the heart as a mistaken stimulus to its virtues; who pay their tribute to great work by belittling human endeavour. Goethe shows us a more excellent way. Touched with a profound feeling of the worth of life, the wisdom of order, the nobility of effort, he gives us an ideal to pursue and shows us the means of pursuing it. Out of the fulness of a large experience, unique in the history of literature, he unfolds the scheme of a practicable perfection, and enforces the lessons he has learned from the steady, passionless, and undaunted observation of human affairs.

To Goethe these sayings were merely reflections or opinions; it is his literary executors and his editors who called them by more ambitious titles, so as to challenge a comparison with certain other famous books of wise thought. They are the reflections of a long life rich in all the intellectual treasures of the world, in its versatility amazing, in its insight well-nigh fathomless; a life that, in his own words, approached the infinite by following the finite on every side.

Such a man need only speak to utter something important; and we on our part need only remember how wide was the range of his knowledge, how full and complete his existence, to set the utmost value on his reflections at the end of it. But that he knew nothing of the pinch of poverty and was spared the horrors of disease, that he suffered no great misfortune, and basked in the bright side of the world, free from the ills that come to most men, there was no page of the book of life that was not thrown open to him. The things of the mind, the things of art, the things of nature—in their theory and in their practice he had worked at them all; regarding them as so many varied manifestations of an eternal Idea in itself inscrutable and here unattainable. There was no kind of literature with which he was unfamiliar, whether it was ancient or modern, of the East or of the West; and the great spiritual influences of the world, Hebraism, Hellenism, Christianity, Mediævalism,—at one or another time in his life he was in touch with them all, and found his account in them all. In matters of learning he was occupied with nothing but what was actual and concrete; it was only to abstract studies, to logic, metaphysics, mathematics, that he was indifferent; in his own phrase, he never thought about thinking. There was hardly any branch of the natural science of his day that he did not cultivate, that he did not himself practise; geology, mineralogy, botany, zoology, anatomy, meteorology, optics; and he made some remarkable discoveries and the strangest prophecies. To Art he gave a life-long devotion. While still a youth, he wrote an important essay on Gothic architecture; he engraved, drew, painted, and for a time took up sculpture. In all the higher forms of Art, with the single exception of music, he had so much practical interest that he often doubted whether in following Literature he had not mistaken, or at least unduly narrowed, the sphere of his activity. He was little abroad, but no one ever profited more by his travels than Goethe. Twice he went to Italy, and what a change of mind was produced by that change of sky! Rome was to him a new birth, a new conception of life. And besides Literature, Science, and Art, he busied himself with Administration, with the duties of the Court, with the practical details of the Theatre; but out of them all he learned something himself and taught something to others. He lived the fullest life granted to man. He had a youth of the wildest enthusiasm and romance; a prime of a classic austerity, of a calm earnestness; a majestic age of the ripest wisdom, when there came to him, as it were a second youth, with something of the fire of the old romantic feeling lighted up in him anew. And out of all these prodigious efforts in so many directions, he passed unharmed, and never lost himself. He steadily pursued his own task and refused to be drawn aside. He stood aloof from the controversies of his time. The battles of belief, philosophical systems, French Revolutions, Wars of Liberation, struggles of democracy and nationality,—these things moved him little or not at all. But he is not on that account to be held, as some foolish critics have held him, indifferent, selfish, or less serious, or less complete a man than his fellows. He did the best in any one's power: he resolutely kept to his own business, and, neither heating nor resting, worked at his own high aims, in the struggle not merely to learn and to know, but to act and to do. He felt profoundly that the best anyone can achieve for himself is often the best he can achieve for others. The whole moral of Wilhelm Meister is that a man's first and greatest duty, whether to others or to himself, is to see that his business in life is a worthy one and suited to his capacities. If he discovers his vocation and pursues it steadily, he will make his outer life of the greatest use and service to the world, and at the same time produce the utmost harmony within. That was what Goethe tried to do in his own person, and he laboured at his self-imposed task with a perseverance, a real unselfishness, and a determination entirely admirable.

It is almost the last fruit of this life of concentrated activity, the final outcome of this indomitable character, that is here put before us. And we shall find that to the complex phenomena of the world Goethe applied no other measure but reason and the nature and needs of man. With a full consciousness of the mysteries that surround our existence, he never made the futile endeavour to pass beyond the bounds of present knowledge and experience, or to resolve contradictions by manipulating the facts. In these detached reflections he does, indeed, propound a theory and sketch out a system of conduct; but they cannot, like the Thoughts of Pascal, for instance, be brought under a single and definite point of view. They are a mirror of life itself, and the inner and outer facts of life in all their diversity. The unity they possess is the unity that is stamped upon them by the all-embracing personality of their author, always and unweariedly striving to make his life systematic, distinct, and fruitful; and to judge them as a whole, a man must be able to fathom so great a genius. But to every one in every walk of life Goethe has a word of wise counsel, as though he understood every form of existence and could enter into its needs. In a fine passage in the Wanderjahre, he likens the thought that thus in wondrous fashion takes a thousand particular shapes, to a mass of quicksilver, which, as it falls, separates into innumerable globules, spreading out on all sides. And while these sayings may present thoughts in seeming contradiction one with another, as the moment that called them forth presented this or that side of experience, their inmost nature is a common tendency to realise a great ideal of life. It is little they owe to the form in which they are cast; they are not the elements of an artistic whole which must be seized before we can understand the full meaning of its parts. They are a miscellaneous record of the shrewdest observation; and to read them as they should be read, a few at a time, is like the opportunity of repeated converse with a man of extraordinary gifts, great insight, and the widest culture, who touches profoundly and suggestively now on this, now on that aspect of life and the world and the progress of knowledge. It is the fruit of his own experience that Goethe gives us; and we shall do well to think of it as he himself thought of another book, and to bear in mind that "every word which we take in a general sense and apply to ourselves, had, under certain circumstances of time and place, a peculiar, special and directly individual references."

Goethe is no exception to the rest of mankind in not being equally wise at all times, and in the maxims there are degrees of value: they do not all shine with the like brilliance. Some of them are valuable only for what they suggest; of some, again, it is easy to see that, they appear as matters of speculation rather than as certainties. They raise difficulties, ask for criticism, if possible, correction; or, it may be, they call attention to the contrary view and invite a harmony of opposites. Some of them make a great demand upon our ability "to understand a proverb and the interpretation; the words of the wise and their dark sayings." Their value sometimes depends on the way they are viewed, the culture brought to their understanding, the temper in which they are approached. We look at them, and at first admire; we change our point of view, and find something to criticise and dispute. The obscurity of maxims, as Goethe reminds us, is only relative; not everything can be explained to the reader which was present to the mind of the writer. Some of them seem at first to be of little interest; on one side they may even repel, but from another they attract again, and win perhaps a partial approval. They seem to move as we change our position, and to be without fixed or certain character. But some, again, are so clear and unmistakable, so immeasurably above criticism or objection, that like the furthest of the stars they have no parallax: whatever position we take, their light is steadfast.

Let no one suppose that in the main Goethe's reflections on life had never been made before; that it was not so, no one knew better than he. As a preface and note of warning to them all, he reiterates the words of the preacher: "there is no new thing under the sun." Yes! says Goethe, there is nothing worth thinking but it has been thought before; we must only try to think it again. "It is only when we are faithful," he says elsewhere,[2] "in arresting and noting our present thoughts, that we have any joy in tradition; since we find the best thoughts already uttered, the finest feelings already expressed. This it is that gives us the perception of that harmonious agreement to which man is called, and to which he must conform, often against his will as he is much too fond of fancying that the world begins afresh with himself." What Goethe means is that we shall do best to find out the truth of all things for ourselves, for on

---

[2] Wilhelm Meisters Wanderjahre, Bk. I. ch. 10.

one side truth is individual; and that we shall be happy if our individual truth is also universal, or accords with the wisest thought of the past. It is in this practical light that we must view the maxims, and not as mere academic generalities. It is easy to read them in an hour and forget them as soon; easy to view them with a tepid interest as the work of a great author; but no one will fully understand the value of any of them, who has not experience enough to know its truth. Well is it for us if with the experience we also gain the truth! If any one should say that some of these maxims are very obvious, and so simply true as almost to be platitudes, I would bid him remember that the best education is often to discover these very simple truths for oneself, and learn to see how much there is in commonplaces. For those who have grown old in the world are never weary of telling us that the further we go, the more we shall find, in general, that the same things will happen to us as have happened to others; and it will then be our advantage if we have the same reflections, best of all if we come of ourselves to the same conclusions, as the wisest of those who have gone before us; next best, if we can really and intelligently follow in the footsteps of their thought.

But although the matter of Goethe's sayings is not original in the sense of being new to the world—while it was original for him, since he discovered it for himself and on his own path, their manner is something new, and their range is unparalleled. Take any other set of maxims you will, nowhere is there so wide an outlook, nowhere so just an estimate of human difficulties, nowhere an aim at once so lofty and so practicable. Nowhere is there a larger, stronger, healthier, more tolerant view of life and the world, or an atmosphere clearer of the mists that too often obscure and distort our vision. And in their expression, nowhere is there so little of the besetting sin to sacrifice truth to effect. Goethe has none of the shallow malice and uncharitable candour that with writers of an earlier age passed for the practical wisdom of every day; and we need only contrast his maxims with the similar work of La Rochefoucauld, Helvetius, and Chamfort, admirable as they may be in their exposure of human selfishness, to determine on which side is the greater service to mankind. How different the views of the world taken by how many writers!—the secret of it all is that the men themselves are different.

It was said of Goethe that his heart, which few knew, was as great as his intellect, which all knew. Certainly his writings and not least his maxims are a profound example of the truth that in the last resort it is moral rather than intellectual qualities that make great literature. It is not to be denied that much may be done by a mere facility of style, a command of words, a fine taste, a wide acquaintance with the turns and resources of language; but in the end the effect is produced by the man himself, his character and his strength. To the strenuous, earnest man, like Goethe, the world offers a stirring spectacle and provides a great opportunity; and he grasps and uses them both to the best of his peculiar capacity. It is diversity of temperament dealing with partial knowledge that makes so many and such various doctrines. A man's views of life are, in short, those which he deserves to have, and his writings are cast in the mould of his character. It is no more strange that the authors of books should give us such varied pictures of the humanity around us, than that painters should conceive natural objects so differently. Literature, too, is like a gallery of landscape and portrait: it is the same world which is presented, the same men and things; but the way of looking at it varies with the artist; who, whatever his training may have been, will see in Nature what he brings to it himself. Ars est homo additus naturæ. If this be truly to define the essence and method of Art, it is equally true to say that Literature is man added to life; and, here as there, everything depends on the character and capacity of the man.

No one has as yet said that he doubts Goethe's capacity, although there are many who have solemnly pronounced him uninteresting. The critic who can read Goethe's works with real attention, and then venture to call them dull, is simply showing that he has no call to the office he assumes, or no interest in literature of the highest class. What is true, of course, is that Goethe is profoundly serious, and he is, therefore, not always entertaining; but that is enough to make him pass for dull in the eyes of those who take literature only as a pastime,—a substitute for a cigar, or something to lull them to sleep when they are tired. But another and more formidable accusation is made against Goethe which affects his character, and would go far to destroy the value of his writings if it were true; but to many it is curiously inconsistent with the other charge of being dull. It is that he is immoral. Now of all the great writers of the world, Goethe is admittedly the greatest teacher. He is essentially and frankly didactic; and nowhere is there so large and worthy a body of literature from a single pen which is informed with so high and so serious a purpose. Roundly to call its author immoral is a charge which sufficiently refutes itself by its own ignorance and absurdity. The charge comes, as a rule, from those who judge life by the needs and duties of a young girl, and they confound the whole of morality—character and conduct in all relations to one's fellow-men—with one section of it. They forget that Goethe was a man of the old régime; that his faults were those of his time and class. They forget that an extreme repugnance to all monasticism, asceticism, and Roman Catholicism in general, naturally led him to pay a diminished regard to the one virtue of which the Christian world is sometimes apt to exaggerate the importance, and on which it is often ready to hang all the law and the prophets. To some, again, Goethe appears to be a supremely selfish wizard, dissecting human passion in the coldest blood, and making poetical capital out of the emotional tortures he caused in others. This, too, is a charge which the merest acquaintance with his life and work must of necessity refute: it is too simple a slander to be seriously discussed. Since these are charges which have, however, kept many estimable people from reading Goethe, it may be some consolation to them to know that the maxims are entirely free from any possibility of objection on this ground.

The element of moral teaching which runs through Goethe's mature works like a golden thread, re-appears in the maxims free and detached from the poetic and romantic environment which in such varied shapes is woven around it in Werther, Tasso, Meister, above all in Faust. To do the next duty; to meet the claims of each day; to persist with a single mind and unwearied effort on a definite, positive, productive path; cheerfully to renounce what is denied us, and vigorously to make the best of what we have; to restrain vague desires and uncertain aims; to cease bewailing the vanity of all things and the fleeting nature of this our world, and do what we can to make our stay in it of lasting use,—these are lessons which will always be needed, and all the more needed as life becomes increasingly complex. They are taught in the maxims with a great variety of application, and nowhere so concisely summarised as in one of them. "The mind endowed with active powers," so it runs, "and keeping with a practical object to the task that lies nearest, is the worthiest there is on earth."

Goethe has been called, and with truth, the prophet of culture; but the word is often misunderstood. We cannot too clearly see that what is here meant is not a mere range of intellectual knowledge, pursued with idolatrous devotion: it is moral discipline, a practical endeavour, forming wise thought and noble character. And this is the product, not of learning, but of work: if we are to know and realise what there is in us, and make the best of it, our aim must be practical and creative. "Let every man," he urges, "ask himself with which of his faculties he can and will somehow influence his age." And again: "From this time forward, if a man does not apply himself to some art or handiwork, he will be in a bad way. In the rapid changes of the world, knowledge is no longer a furtherance. By the time a man has taken note of everything, he has lost himself." The culture of which he speaks is not mainly intellectual. We use the word in a way that is apt to limit and conceal its meaning, and we often apply it to a strange form of mental growth, at once stunted and overfed, to which, if we may judge by its fruits, any breath of real culture would be fatal. It has nothing to do with learning in the general and narrow sense of the word, or with the often pernicious effects of mere learning. In the language of the hour we are wont to give the exclusive name of culture to a wide acquaintance with books and languages; whether or not it results, as it has before now resulted, in a want of culture in character and outward demeanour, in airs of conceit, in foolish arrogance, in malice and acrimony.

A uniform activity with a moral aim—that, in Goethe's view, is the highest we can achieve in life. "Character in matters great and small consists," he says, "in a man steadily pursuing the things of which he feels himself capable." It is the gospel of work: our endeavour must be to realise our best self in deed and action; to strive until our personality attains, in Aristotle's word, its entelechy; its full development. By this alone can we resolve all the doubts and hesitations and conflicts within that undermine and destroy the soul. "Try to do your duty, and you will know at once what you are worth." And with all our doing, what should be the goal of our activity? In no wise our own self, our own weal. "A man is happy only when he delights in the good-will of others," and we must of a truth "give up existence in order to exist"; we must never suppose that happiness is identical with personal welfare. In the moral sphere we need, as Kant taught, a categorical imperative; but, says Goethe, that is not the end of the matter; it is only the beginning. We must widen our conception of duty and recognise a perfect morality only "where a man loves what he commands himself to do." "Voluntary dependence is the best state, and how should that be possible without love?" And just in the same sense Goethe refuses to regard all self-denial as virtuous, but only the self-denial that leads to some useful end. All other forms of it are immoral, since they stunt and cramp the free development of what is best in us—the desire, namely, to deal effectively with our present life, and make the most and fairest of it.

And here it is that Goethe's moral code is fused with his religious belief. "Piety," he says, "is not an end but a means: a means of attaining the highest culture by the purest tranquillity of soul." This is the piety he preaches; not the morbid introspection that leads to no useful end, the state of brooding melancholy, the timorous self-abasement, the anxious speculation as to some other condition of being. And this tranquillity of soul, Goethe taught that it should be ours, in spite of the thousand ills of life which give us pause in our optimism. It is attained by the firm assurance that, somewhere and somehow, a power exists that makes for moral good; that our moral endeavours are met, so to speak, half-way by a moral order in the universe, which comes to the aid of individual effort. And the sum and substance of his teaching, whether in the maxims or in any other of his mature productions, is that we must resign ourselves to this power, in gratitude and reverence towards it and all its manifestations in whatever is good and beautiful. This is Goethe's strong faith, his perfect and serene trust. He finely shadows it forth in the closing words of Pandora, where Eos proclaims that the work of the gods is to lead our efforts to the eternal good, and that we must give them free play:—

> Was zu wünschen ist, ihr unten fühlt es;
> Was zu geben sei, die wissen's droben.
> Gross beginnet ihr Titanen; aber leiten
> Zu dem ewig Guten, ewig Schönen,
> Ist der Götter Werk; die lasst gewähren.

And so too in Faust: it is the long struggle to realise an Ideal, dimly seen on life's labyrinthine way of error, that leads at last to the perfect redemption:—

> Wer immer strebend sich bemüht,
> Den können wir erlösen.

And throughout the perplexities of life and the world, where all things are but signs and tokens of some inner and hidden reality, it is the ideal of love and service, das Ewig-Weibliche, that draws us on.

But this assurance cannot be reached by a mere theory; and Goethe is not slow to declare how he views attempts to reach it in that way. "Credo Deum! that," he reminds us here, "is a fine, a worthy thing to say; but to recognise God when and where he reveals himself, is the only true bliss on earth." All else is mystery. We are not born, as he said to Eckermann, to solve the problems of the world, but to find out where the problem begins, and then to keep within the limits of what we can grasp. The problem, he urged, is transformed into a postulate: if we cannot get a solution theoretically, we can get it in the experience of practical life. We reach it by the use of an "active scepticism," of which he says that "it continually aims at overcoming itself and arriving by means of regulated experience at a kind of conditioned certainty." But he would have nothing to do with doctrinal systems, and, like Schiller, professed none of the forms of religion from a feeling of religion itself. To see how he views some particular questions of theology the reader may turn with profit to his maxims on the Reformation and early Christianity, and to his admirable remarks on the use and abuse of the Bible. The basis of religion was for him its own earnestness; and it was not always needful, he held, for truth to take a definite shape: "it is enough if it hovers about us like a spirit and produces harmony." "I believe," he said to Eckermann, "in God and Nature and the victory of good over evil; but I was also asked to believe that three was one, and one was three. That jarred upon my feeling for truth; and I did not see how it could have helped me in the least." As for letting our minds roam beyond this present life, he thought there was actual danger in it; although he looked for a future existence, a continuation of work and activity, in which what is here incomplete should reach its full development. And whatever be the secrets of the universe, assuredly the best we can do is to do our best here; and the worst of blasphemies is to regard this life as altogether vanity; for as these pages tell us, "it would not be worth while to see seventy years if all the wisdom of this world were foolishness with God."

In Goethe we pass, as over a bridge, from the eighteenth century to the nineteenth; but though he lived to see a third of the nineteenth century, he hardly belongs to it. Of its political characteristics he had few or none. He was no democrat. As the prophet of inward culture, he took the French Revolution for a disturbance, an interruption, and not a development in the progress of the world's history; and for all its horrors and the pernicious demoralisation of its leaders, he had the profoundest aversion. But afterwards he came to see that it had beneficial results; that a revolution is ultimately never the fault of the people, but of the injustice and incapacity of the government; and that where there is a real necessity for a great reform, the old leaven must be rooted out.[3] But he knew the danger of such a process, and he indicates it here in an admirable saying: "Before the French Revolution it was all effort; afterwards it all changed to demand"; and this may be supplemented by his opinion on the nature of revolutionary sentiments: "Men think they would be well-off if they were not ruled, and fail to perceive that they can rule neither themselves nor others." And if he, had thus no theoretical sympathy with democratic movements, he had little feeling for that other great political tendency of our time—nationality; convinced as he was that interest in the weal and woe of another people is always a mark of the highest culture. But apart from politics there is one characteristic of our own time in which he fully and especially shares, if only for the reason that he did much himself to produce it; and herein he has influenced us profoundly and is influencing us still. The nineteenth century has this advantage over every preceding age, that in it for the first time honest doubt, instead of distinguishing a few, has become a common virtue. Goethe is one of the surest and safest of those who have led the transition. "We praise the eighteenth century," he writes, "for concerning itself chiefly with analysis. The task remaining to the nineteenth is to discover the false syntheses which prevail, and to analyse their contents anew." Of the aim of analysis and the proper course of inquiry, no one has given a better account than Goethe in what he says, in the words I have quoted, about active scepticism; and in the sphere of morals and religion it will perhaps be found hereafter that he has contributed, in some degree at least, to the attainment of that "conditioned certainty," for which, as we hope, all our efforts are made.

---

[3] Gespräche mit Eckermann, III. 4 January, 1824.

In the maxims on Literature there is some excellent criticism on literary methods, and much that may well be taken to heart by certain writers of our own day. Goethe had little but rebuke for the whole of the romantic movement, which began in his old age. The German form of it he thought unnatural, and at best a conventional imitation of an earlier period; and the French form, of which Victor Hugo was then the rising star, he thought a perversion of naturalism, an exaggeration of it until it became insipid or merely revolting. To Byron alone he gave the tribute of the most ungrudging admiration: in the opposition between classicism and romanticism, he declined to take him for a follower of either, but as the complete representative of his own time. The maxim that "the classical is health, and the romantic, disease," may not altogether commend itself to us now; but with wonderful insight Goethe foresaw the direction in which the romantic movement would lead. "The romantic," he says here, "is already fallen into its own abysm. It is hard to imagine anything more degraded than the worst of the new productions." If he could have said this two generations ago, what would he have said now? How could he have spoken without contempt of those who make all that is common and unclean in itself a subject with which literature may properly be occupied? These are the writers who profess to be realists, under a completely mistaken notion of what realism means, as applied to art; and to them the chief realities seem to be just the very things that decent people keep out of sight. They forget that in literature, as in all art, the dominating realities are the highest Ideals. As an antidote to this poison of corruption Goethe pointed to the ancient world, and bid us study there the types of the loftiest manhood. "Bodies which rot while they are still alive and are edified by the detailed contemplation of their own decay; dead men who remain in the world for the ruin of others, and feed their death on the living—to this," he exclaimed, "have come our makers of literature. When the same thing happened in antiquity, it was only as a strange token of some rare disease; but with the moderns the disease has become endemic and epidemic." Akin to these pseudo-realists, and coming under the same ban, are some of our modern novel-writers who do, indeed, avoid the depth of degradation, but try to move the feelings by dwelling in a similar fashion on matters which are not, and never can be, fit subjects of literary treatment; such as painful deaths by horrible distempers, or the minute details of prolonged operations. It is poor skill that cannot find material enough in the moral sufferings of men and women, and is driven to seek effect in descriptions of disease and surgery. Surely in any literature worthy of the name these are topics which a richer imagination and a more prolific art would have found unnecessary, and better taste would have left undescribed.

To another class of writers—those who handle a pretty pen without having anything definite to present, or anything important to say, Goethe has also an applicable word. It is a class which is always increasing in number, and tends to increase in talent. We may admit that second- or third-rate work, especially in poetry, was never before done so well as it is done now; and still we may find some useful truth in a distinction which Goethe drew for the benefit of the minor poets and the minor prose-writers of his own age. "Productions are now possible," he said, "which, without being bad, have no value. They have no value, because they contain nothing; and they are not bad, because a general form of good workmanship is present to the author's mind." In one of the many neglected volumes of his miscellaneous writings Goethe has a series of admirable notes for a proposed work on Dilettantism; and there the reader, if he is interested in Goethe's literary criticism, will find some instructive remarks in close connection with this aphorism, and also certain rules for discriminating between good and indifferent work which ought to receive the most attentive study. And the stylists who neglect plain language for a mosaic of curious phrase and overstrained epithet, may profitably remember that, as Goethe here says, "it is not language in itself which is correct or forcible or elegant, but the mind that is embodied in it."

"Translators," he tells us, "sing the praises of some half-veiled beauty and rouse an irresistible longing for the original." To them also he gives a piece of excellent advice: "The translator must proceed until he reaches the untranslatable." This is a counsel of exhortation as well as of warning. It bids the translator spare no effort, but tells him that at a certain point his efforts are of no avail. But none the less, Goethe might have added, the faithful translator must strive as if this hindrance to perfection did not exist; for it is thus only that he, or any one else, can do anything worth doing. On methods of translation much may be said, and it is sometimes urged, in a given case, that it is not literal or that it is too free. A distinguished writer has recently laid down that a translation should reproduce every word and phrase and sentence of the original as accurately as a delicate tracing reproduces the lines of a drawing. This is advice which may hold in the school-room, but, I venture to maintain, nowhere else. In so far as every language has a peculiar genius, a literal translation must necessarily be a bad one; and any faithful translation will of its nature be free. In other words, a translator will err if he slavishly adheres to mere expression; he must have complete liberty to give his author's meaning and style in the manner which he holds to be truest to the original; and so, in translating from a foreign tongue, it will be well for him to have some knowledge of his own. But he must guard against the abuse of his position: his liberty may become license, and his translation instead of being faithful may be phantastic. The translator's first and last duty is, then, to efface himself. His first duty is to stand entirely at the point of view of his author's thought; his last, to find the clearest and nearest expression in his own language both for that thought and for whatever is characteristic in the way of conveying it; neither adding anything of his own nor taking away anything from his author. The best translation is thus a re-embodiment of the author's spirit, a real metempsychosis. Nothing can be done without ideals, and this is the ideal at which the present translation aims. That it fails of its aim and has many defects, no one knows better than the translator himself; and he can only cherish the hope that where he falls short he is sometimes close to the confines of what cannot be translated.

Bailey Saunders

LIFE AND CHARACTER

I

1

There is nothing worth thinking but it has been thought before; we must only try to think it again.

2

How can a man come to know himself? Never by thinking, but by doing. Try to do your duty, and you will know at once what you are worth.

3

But what is your duty? The claims of the day.

4

The world of reason is to be regarded as a great and immortal being, who ceaselessly works out what is necessary, and so makes himself lord also over what is accidental.

5

The longer I live, the more it grieves me to see man, who occupies his supreme place for the very purpose of imposing his will upon nature, and freeing himself and his from an outrageous necessity,—

to see him taken up with some false notion, and doing just the opposite of what he wants to do; and then, because the whole bent of his mind is spoilt, bungling miserably over everything.

6

Be genuine and strenuous; earn for yourself, and look for, grace from those in high places; from the powerful, favour; from the active and the good, advancement; from the many, affection; from the individual, love.

7

Tell me with whom you associate, and I will tell you who you are. If I know what your business is, I know what can be made of you.

8

Every man must think after his own fashion; for on his own path he finds a truth, or a kind of truth, which helps him through life. But he must not give himself the rein; he must control himself; mere naked instinct does not become him.

9

Unqualified activity, of whatever kind, leads at last to bankruptcy.

10

In the works of mankind, as in those of nature, it is really the motive which is chiefly worth attention.

11

Men get out of countenance with themselves and others because they treat the means as the end, and so, from sheer doing, do nothing, or, perhaps, just what they would have avoided.

12

Our plans and designs should be so perfect in truth and beauty, that in touching them the world could only mar. We should thus have the advantage of setting right what is wrong, and restoring what is destroyed.

13

It is a very hard and troublesome thing to dispose of whole, half-, and quarter-mistakes; to sift them and assign the portion of truth to its proper place.

14

It is not always needful for truth to take a definite shape; it is enough if it hovers about us like a spirit and produces harmony; if it is wafted through the air like the sound of a bell, grave and kindly.

15

General ideas and great conceit are always in a fair way to bring about terrible misfortune.

You cannot play the flute by blowing alone: you must use your fingers.

In Botany there is a species of plants called Incompletæ; and just in the same way it can be said that there are men who are incomplete and imperfect. They are those whose desires and struggles are out of proportion to their actions and achievements.

The most insignificant man can be complete if he works within the limits of his capacities, innate or acquired; but even fine talents can be obscured, neutralised, and destroyed by lack of this indispensable requirement of symmetry. This is a mischief which will often occur in modern times; for who will be able to come up to the claims of an age so full and intense as this, and one too that moves so rapidly?

It is only men of practical ability, knowing their powers and using them with moderation and prudence, who will be successful in worldly affairs.

It is a great error to take oneself for more than one is, or for less than one is worth.

21

From time to time I meet with a youth in whom I can wish for no alteration or improvement, only I am sorry to see how often his nature makes him quite ready to swim with the stream of the time; and it is on this that I would always insist, that man in his fragile boat has the rudder placed in his hand, just that he may not be at the mercy of the waves, but follow the direction of his own insight.

22

But how is a young man to come of himself to see blame in things which every one is busy with, which every one approves and promotes? Why should he not follow his natural bent and go in the same direction as they?

23

I must hold it for the greatest calamity of our time, which lets nothing come to maturity, that one moment is consumed by the next, and the day spent in the day; so that a man is always living from hand to mouth, without having anything to show for it. Have we not already newspapers for every hour of the day! A good head could assuredly intercalate one or other of them. They publish abroad everything that every one does, or is busy with or meditating; nay, his very designs are thereby dragged into publicity. No one can rejoice or be sorry, but as a pastime for others; and so it goes on from house to house, from city to city, from kingdom to kingdom, and at last from one hemisphere to the other, — all in post haste.

As little as you can stifle a steam-engine, so little can you do this in the moral sphere either. The activity of commerce, the rush and rustle of paper-money, the swelling-up of debts to pay debts—all these are the monstrous elements to which in these days a young man is exposed. Well is it for him if he is gifted by nature with a sober, quiet temperament; neither to make claims on the world out of all proportion to his position, nor yet let the world determine it.

But on all sides he is threatened by the spirit of the day, and nothing is more needful than to make him see early enough the direction in which his will has to steer.

The significance of the most harmless words and actions grows with the years, and if I see any one about me for any length of time, I always try to show him the difference there is between sincerity, confidence, and indiscretion; nay, that in truth there is no difference at all, but a gentle transition from what is most innocent to what is most hurtful; a transition which must be perceived or rather felt.

Herein we must exercise our tact; otherwise in the very way in which we have won the favour of mankind, we run the risk of trifling it away again unawares. This is a lesson which a man learns quite well for himself in the course of life, but only after having paid a dear price for it; nor can he, unhappily, spare his posterity a like expenditure.

28

Love of truth shows itself in this, that a man knows how to find and value the good in everything.

29

Character calls forth character.

30

If I am to listen to another man's opinion, it must be expressed positively. Of things problematical I have enough in myself.

31

Superstition is a part of the very being of humanity; and when we fancy that we are banishing it altogether, it takes refuge in the strangest nooks and corners, and then suddenly comes forth again, as soon as it believes itself at all safe.

32

I keep silence about many things, for I do not want to put people out of countenance; and I am well content if they are pleased with things that annoy me.

33

Everything that frees our spirit without giving us control of ourselves is ruinous.

A man is really alive only when he delights in the good-will of others.

Piety is not an end, but a means: a means of attaining the highest culture by the purest tranquillity of soul.

Hence it may be observed that those who set up piety as an end and object are mostly hypocrites.

When a man is old he must do more than when he was young.

To fulfil a duty is still always to feel it as a debt, for it is never quite satisfying to oneself.

Defects are perceived only by one who has no love; therefore, to see them, a man must become uncharitable, but not more so than is necessary for the purpose.

40

The greatest piece of good fortune is that which corrects our deficiencies and redeems our mistakes.

41

Reading ought to mean understanding; writing ought to mean knowing something; believing ought to mean comprehending; when you desire a thing, you will have to take it; when you demand it, you will not get it; and when you are experienced, you ought to be useful to others.

42

The stream is friendly to the miller whom it serves; it likes to pour over the mill wheels; what is the good of it stealing through the valley in apathy?

43

Whoso is content with pure experience and acts upon it has enough of truth. The growing child is wise in this sense.

44

Theory is in itself of no use, except in so far as it makes us believe in the connection of phenomena.

When a man asks too much and delights in complication, he is exposed to perplexity.

Thinking by means of analogies is not to be condemned. Analogy has this advantage, that it comes to no conclusion, and does not, in truth, aim at finality at all. Induction, on the contrary, is fatal, for it sets up an object and keeps it in view, and, working on towards it, drags false and true with it in its train.

The absent works upon us by tradition. The usual form of it may be called historical; a higher form, akin to the imaginative faculty, is the mythical. If some third form of it is to be sought behind this last, and it has any meaning, it is transformed into the mystical. It also easily becomes sentimental, so that we appropriate to our use only what suits us.

In contemplation as in action, we must distinguish between what may be attained and what is unattainable. Without this, little can be achieved, either in life or in knowledge.

'Le sense commun est le génie de l'humanité.'

Common-sense, which is here put forward as the genius of

humanity, must be examined first of all in the way it shows itself. If we inquire the purpose to which humanity puts it, we find as follows: Humanity is conditioned by needs. If they are not satisfied, men become impatient; and if they are, it seems not to affect them. The normal man moves between these two states, and he applies his understanding—his so-called common-sense—to the satisfaction of his needs. When his needs are satisfied, his task is to fill up the waste spaces of indifference. Here, too, he is successful, if his needs are confined to what is nearest and most necessary. But if they rise and pass beyond the sphere of ordinary wants, common-sense is no longer sufficient; it is a genius no more, and humanity enters on the region of error.

50

There is no piece of foolishness but it can be corrected by intelligence or accident; no piece of wisdom but it can miscarry by lack of intelligence or by accident.

51

Every great idea is a tyrant when it first appears; hence the advantages which it produces change all too quickly into disadvantages. It is possible, then, to defend and praise any institution that exists, if its beginnings are brought to remembrance, and it is shown that everything which was true of it at the beginning is true of it still.

52

Lessing, who chafed under the sense of various limitations, makes one of his characters say: No one must do anything. A clever pious man said: If a man wills something, he must do it. A third, who was, it is true, an educated man, added: Will follows upon insight. The whole circle of knowledge, will, and necessity was thus believed to have been completed. But, as a rule, a man's knowledge, of whatever kind it may be, determines what he shall do and what he shall leave undone, and so it is that there is no more terrible sight than ignorance in action.

53

There are two powers that make for peace: what is right, and what is fitting.

54

Justice insists on obligation, law on decorum. Justice weighs and decides, law superintends and orders. Justice refers to the individual, law to society.

55

The history of knowledge is a great fugue in which the voices of the nations one after the other emerge.

II

56

If a man is to achieve all that is asked of him, he must take himself for more than he is, and as long as he does not carry it to an absurd length, we willingly put up with it.

57

Work makes companionship.

58

People whip curds to see if they cannot make cream of them.

59

It is much easier to put yourself in the position of a mind taken up with the most absolute error, than of one which mirrors to itself half-truths.

60

Wisdom lies only in truth.

61

When I err, every one can see it; but not when I lie.

62

Is not the world full enough of riddles already, without our making riddles too out of the simplest phenomena?

63

'The finest hair throws a shadow.' Erasmus.

64

What I have tried to do in my life through false tendencies, I have at last learned to understand.

65

Generosity wins favour for every one, especially when it is accompanied by modesty.

66

Before the storm breaks, the dust rises violently for the last time — the dust that is soon to be laid forever.

67

Men do not come to know one another easily, even with the best will and the best purpose. And then ill-will comes in and distorts everything.

68

We should know one another better if one man were not so anxious to put himself on an equality with another.

69

Eminent men are therefore in a worse plight than others; for, as we cannot compare ourselves with them, we are on the watch for them.

70

In the world the point is, not to know men, but at any given moment to be cleverer than the man who stands before you. You can prove this at every fair and from every charlatan.

71

Not everywhere where there is water, are there frogs; but where you have frogs, there you will find water.

72

Error is quite right as long as we are young, but we must not carry it on with us into our old age.

Whims and eccentricities that grow stale are all useless, rank nonsense.

73

In the formation of species Nature gets, as it were, into a cul-de-sac;

she cannot make her way through, and is disinclined to turn back. Hence the stubbornness of national character.

74

Every one has something in his nature which, if he were to express it openly, would of necessity give offence.

75

If a man thinks about his physical or moral condition, he generally finds that he is ill.

76

Nature asks that a man should sometimes be stupefied without going to sleep; hence the pleasure in the smoking of tobacco, the drinking of brandy, the use of opiates.

77

The man who is up and doing should see to it that what he does is right. Whether or not right is done, is a matter which should not trouble him.

78

Many a man knocks about on the wall with his hammer, and believes that he hits the right nail on the head every time.

79

Painting and tattooing of the body is a return to animalism.

80

History-writing is a way of getting rid of the past.

81

What a man does not understand, he does not possess.

82

Not every one who has a pregnant thought delivered to him becomes productive; it probably makes him think of something with which he is quite familiar.

83

Favour, as a symbol of sovereignty, is exercised by weak men.

84

Every man has enough power left to carry out that of which he is convinced.

85

Memory may vanish so long as at the moment judgment does not fail you.

86

No nation gains the power of judgment except it can pass judgment on itself. But to attain this great privilege takes a very long time.

87

Instead of contradicting my words people ought to act in my spirit.

88

Those who oppose intellectual truths do but stir up the fire, and the cinders fly about and burn what they had else not touched.

89

Man would not be the finest creature in the world if he were not too fine for it.

90

What a long time people were vainly disputing about the Antipodes!

91

Certain minds must be allowed their peculiarities.

92

Snow is false purity.

93

Whoso shrinks from ideas ends by having nothing but sensations.

94

Those from whom we are always learning are rightly called our masters; but not every one who teaches us deserves this title.

95

It is with you as with the sea: the most varied names are given to what is in the end only salt water.

96

It is said that vain self-praise stinks in the nostrils. That may be so; but for the kind of smell which comes from unjust blame by others the public has no nose at all.

97

There are problematical natures which are equal to no position in which they find themselves, and which no position satisfies. This it is that causes that hideous conflict which wastes life and deprives it of all pleasure.

98

If we do any real good, it is mostly clam, vi, et precario.

99

Dirt glitters as long as the sun shines.

100

It is difficult to be just to the passing moment. We are bored by it if it is neither good nor bad; but the good moment lays a task upon us, and the bad moment a burden.

101

He is the happiest man who can set the end of his life in connection with the beginning.

102

So obstinately contradictory is man that you cannot compel him to his advantage, yet he yields before everything that forces him to his hurt.

103

Forethought is simple, afterthought manifold.

104

A state of things in which every day brings some new trouble is not the right one.

105

When people suffer by failing to look before them, nothing is commoner than trying to look out for some possible remedy.

106

The Hindoos of the Desert make a solemn vow to eat no fish.

107

To venture an opinion is like moving a piece at chess: it may be taken, but it forms the beginning of a game that is won.

108

It is as certain as it is strange that truth and error come from one and the same source. Thus it is that we are often not at liberty to do violence to error, because at the same time we do violence to truth.

109

Truth belongs to the man, error to his age. This is why it has been said that, while the misfortune of the age caused his error, the force of his soul made him emerge from the error with glory.

110

Every one has his peculiarities and cannot get rid of them; and yet many a one is destroyed by his peculiarities, and those too of the most innocent kind.

111

If a man does think too much of himself, he is more than he believes himself to be.

112

In art and knowledge, as also in deed and action, everything depends on a pure apprehension of the object and a treatment of it according to its nature.

113

When intelligent and sensible people despise knowledge in their old age, it is only because they have asked too much of it and of themselves.

114

I pity those who make much ado about the transitory nature of all things and are lost in the contemplation of earthly vanity: are we not here to make the transitory permanent? This we can do only if we know how to value both.

115

A rainbow which lasts a quarter of an hour is looked at no more.

116

It used to happen, and still happens, to me to take no pleasure in a work of art at the first sight of it, because it is too much for me; but if I suspect any merit in it, I try to get at it; and then I never fail to make the most gratifying discoveries, — to find new qualities in the work itself and new faculties in myself.

117

Faith is private capital, kept in one's own house. There are public savings-banks and loan-offices, which supply individuals in their day of need; but here the creditor quietly takes his interest for himself.

118

Real obscurantism is not to hinder the spread of what is true, clear, and useful, but to bring into vogue what is false.

119

During a prolonged study of the lives of various men both great and small, I came upon this thought: In the web of the world the one may well be regarded as the warp, the other as the woof. It is the little men, after all, who give breadth to the web, and the great men firmness and solidity; perhaps, also, the addition of some sort of pattern. But the scissors of the Fates determine its length, and to that all the rest must join in submitting itself.

120

Truth is a torch, but a huge one, and so it is only with blinking eyes that we all of us try to get past it, in actual terror of being burnt.

'The wise have much in common with one another.' Æschylus.

122

The really foolish thing in men who are otherwise intelligent is that they fail to understand what another person says, when he does not exactly hit upon the right way of saying it.

123

Because a man speaks, he thinks he is able to speak about language.

124

One need only grow old to become gentler in one's judgments. I see no fault committed which I could not have committed myself.

125

The man who acts never has any conscience; no one has any conscience but the man who thinks.

126

Why should those who are happy expect one who is miserable to die before them in a graceful attitude, like the gladiator before the Roman mob?

127

Some one asked Timon about the education of his children. 'Let them,' he said, 'be instructed in that which they will never understand.'

128

There are people whom I wish well, and would that I could wish better.

129

By force of habit we look at a clock that has run down as if it were still going, and we gaze at the face of a beauty as though she still loved.

130

Hatred is active displeasure, envy passive. We need not wonder that envy turns so soon to hatred.

131

There is something magical in rhythm; it even makes us believe that we possess the sublime.

132

Dilettantism treated seriously, and knowledge pursued mechanically, end by becoming pedantry.

133

No one but the master can promote the cause of Art. Patrons help the master,—that is right and proper; but that does not always mean that Art is helped.

134

The most foolish of all errors is for clever young men to believe that they forfeit their originality in recognising a truth which has already been recognised by others.

135

Scholars are generally malignant when they are refuting others; and if they think a man is making a mistake, they straightway look upon him as their mortal enemy.

136

Beauty can never really understand itself.

III

137

It is much easier to recognise error than to find truth; for error lies on the surface and may be overcome; but truth lies in the depths, and to search for it is not given to every one.

138

We all live on the past, and through the past are destroyed.

139

We are no sooner about to learn some great lesson than we take refuge in our own innate poverty of soul, and yet for all that the lesson has not been quite in vain.

140

The world of empirical morality consists for the most part of nothing but ill-will and envy.

141

Life seems so vulgar, so easily content with the commonplace things of every day, and yet it always nurses and cherishes certain higher claims in secret, and looks about for the means of satisfying them.

142

Confidences are strange things. If you listen only to one man, it is possible that he is deceived or mistaken; if you listen to many, they are in a like case; and, generally, you cannot get at the truth at all.

143

No one should desire to live in irregular circumstances; but if by chance a man falls into them, they test his character and show of how much determination he is capable.

144

An honourable man with limited ideas often sees through the rascality of the most cunning jobber.

145

If a man feels no love, he must learn how to flatter; otherwise he will not succeed.

146

Against criticism a man can neither protest nor defend himself; he must act in spite of it, and then criticism will gradually yield to him.

147

The masses cannot dispense with men of ability, and such men are always a burden to them.

148

If a man spreads my failings abroad, he is my master, even though he were my servant.

149

Whether memoirs are written by masters of servants, or by servants of masters, the processes always meet.

150

If you lay duties upon people and give them no rights, you must pay them well.

151

I can promise to be sincere, but not to be impartial.

152

Ingratitude is always a kind of weakness. I have never known men of ability to be ungrateful.

153

We are all so limited that we always think we are right; and so we may conceive of an extraordinary mind which not only errs but has a positive delight in error.

154

It is very rare to find pure and steady activity in the accomplishment of what is good and right. We usually see pedantry trying to keep back, and audacity trying to go on too fast.

155

Word and picture are correlatives which are continually in quest of each other, as is sufficiently evident in the case of metaphors and similes. So from all time what was said or sung inwardly to the ear had to be presented equally to the eye. And so in childish days we see word and picture in continual balance; in the book of the law and in the way of salvation, in the Bible and in the spelling-book. When something was spoken which could not be pictured, and something pictured which could not be spoken, all went well; but mistakes were often made, and a word was used instead of a picture; and thence arose those monsters of symbolical mysticism, which are doubly an evil.

156

For the man of the world a collection of anecdotes and maxims is of the greatest value, if he knows how to intersperse the one in his conversation at fitting moments, and remember the other when a case arises for their application.

157

When you lose interest in anything, you also lose the memory for it.

158

The world is a bell with a crack in it; it rattles, but does not ring.

159

The importunity of young dilettanti must be borne with good-will; for as they grow old they become the truest worshippers of Art and the Master.

160

People have to become really bad before they care for nothing but mischief, and delight in it.

161

Clever people are the best encyclopædia.

162

There are people who make no mistakes because they never wish to do anything worth doing.

163

If I know my relation to myself and the outer world, I call it truth. Every man can have his own peculiar truth; and yet it is always the same.

164

No one is the master of any truly productive energy; and all men must let it work on by itself.

165

A man never understands how anthropomorphic he is.

166

A difference which offers nothing to the understanding is no difference at all.

167

A man cannot live for every one; least of all for those with whom he would not care to live.

168

If a man sets out to study all the laws, he will have no time left to transgress them.

169

Things that are mysterious are not yet miracles.

170

'Converts are not in my good books.'

171

A frivolous impulsive encouragement of problematical talents was a mistake of my early years; and I have never been able to abandon it altogether.

172

I should like to be honest with you, without our falling out; but it will not do. You act wrongly, and fall between two stools; you win no adherents and lose your friends. What is to be the end of it?

173

It is all one whether you are of high or of humble origin. You will always have to pay for your humanity.

174

When I hear people speak of liberal ideas, it is always a wonder to me that men are so readily put off with empty verbiage. An idea cannot be liberal; but it may be potent, vigorous, exclusive, in order to fulfil its mission of being productive. Still less can a concept be liberal; for a concept has quite another mission. Where, however, we must look for liberality, is in the sentiments; and the sentiments are the inner man as he lives and moves. A man's sentiments, however, are rarely liberal, because they proceed directly from him personally, and from his immediate relations and requirements. Further we will not write, and let us apply this test to what we hear every day.

175

If a clever man commits a folly, it is not a small one.

176

There is a poetry without figures of speech, which is a single figure of speech.

177

I went on troubling myself about general ideas until I learnt to understand the particular achievements of the best men.

178

It is only when a man knows little, that he knows anything at all. With knowledge grows doubt.

179

The errors of a man are what make him really lovable.

180

There are men who love their like and seek it; others love their opposite and follow after it.

181

If a man has always let himself think the world as bad as the adversary represents it to be, he must have become a miserable person.

182

Ill-favour and hatred limit the spectator to the surface, even when keen perception is added unto them; but when keen perception unites with good-will and love, it gets at the heart of man and the world; nay, it may hope to reach the highest goal of all.

183

Raw matter is seen by every one; the contents are found only by him who has his eyes about him; and the form is a secret to the majority.

184

We may learn to know the world as we please: it will always retain a bright and a dark side.

185

Error is continually repeating itself in action, and we must unweariedly repeat the truth in word.

186

As in Rome there is, apart from the Romans, a population of statues, so apart from this real world there is a world of illusion, almost more potent, in which most men live.

187

Mankind is like the Red Sea: the staff has scarcely parted the waves asunder, before they flow together again.

188

Thoughts come back; beliefs persist; facts pass by never to return.

189

Of all peoples, the Greeks have dreamt the dream of life the best.

190

We readily bow to antiquity, but not to posterity. It is only a father that does not grudge talent to his son.

191

There is no virtue in subordinating oneself; but there is virtue in descending, and in recognising anything as above us, which is beneath us.

192

The whole art of living consists in giving up existence in order to exist.

193

All our pursuits and actions are a wearying process. Well is it for him who wearies not.

194

Hope is the second soul of the unhappy.

195

Love is a true renovator.

196

Mankind is not without a wish to serve; hence the chivalry of the French is a servitude.

197

In the theatre the pleasure of what we see and hear restrains our reflections.

198

There is no limit to the increase of experience, but theories cannot become clearer and more complete in just the same sense. The field of experience is the whole universe in all directions. Theory remains shut up within the limits of the human faculties. Hence there is no way of looking at the world, but it recurs, and the curious thing happens, that with increased experience a limited theory may again come into favour.

It is always the same world which stands open to observation, which is continually being contemplated or guessed at; and it is always the same men who live in the true or in the false; more at their ease in the latter than in the former.

199

Truth is at variance with our natures, but not so error; and for a very simple reason. Truth requires us to recognise ourselves as limited, but error flatters us with the belief that in one way or another we are subject to no bounds at all.

200

That some men think they can still do what they have been able to do, is natural enough; that others think they can do what they have never been able to do, is singular, but not rare.

201

At all times it has not been the age, but individuals alone, who have worked for knowledge. It was the age which put Socrates to death by poison, the age which burnt Huss. The ages have always remained alike.

202

That is true Symbolism, where the more particular represents the more general, not as a dream or shade, but as a vivid, instantaneous revelation of the Inscrutable.

Everything of an abstract or symbolic nature, as soon as it is challenged by realities, ends by consuming them and itself. So credit consumes both money and itself.

204

Mastery often passes for egoism.

205

With Protestants, as soon as good works cease and their merit is denied, sentimentality takes their place.

206

If a man knows where to get good advice, it is as though he could supply it himself.

207

The use of mottoes is to indicate something we have not attained, but strive to attain. It is right to keep them always before our eyes.

208

'If a man cannot lift a stone himself, let him leave it, even though he has some one to help him.'

209

Despotism promotes general self-government, because from top to bottom it makes the individual responsible, and so produces the highest degree of activity.

210

A man must pay dear for his errors if he wishes to get rid of them, and even then he is lucky.

211

Enthusiasm is of the greatest value, so long as we are not carried away by it.

212

School itself is the only true preparation for it.

213

Error is related to truth as sleep to waking. I have observed that on awakening from error a man turns again to truth as with new vigour.

214

Every one suffers who does not work for himself. A man works for others to have them share in his joy.

215

Men's prejudices rest upon their character for the time being and cannot be overcome, as being part and parcel of themselves. Neither evidence nor common-sense nor reason has the slightest influence upon them.

216

Characters often make a law of their failings. Men who know the world have said that when prudence is only fear in disguise, its scruples cannot be conquered. The weak often have revolutionary sentiments; they think they would be well off if they were not ruled, and fail to perceive that they can rule neither themselves nor others.

217

Common-sense is born pure in the healthy man, is self-developed, and is revealed by a resolute perception and recognition of what is necessary and useful. Practical men and women avail themselves of it with confidence. Where it is absent, both sexes find anything necessary when they desire it, and useful when it gives them pleasure.

218

All men, as they attain freedom, give play to their errors. The strong do too much, and the weak too little.

219

The conflict of the old, the existing, the continuing, with

development, improvement, and reform, is always the same. Order of every kind turns at last to pedantry, and to get rid of the one, people destroy the other; and so it goes on for a while, until people perceive that order must be established anew. Classicism and Romanticism; close corporations and freedom of trade; the maintenance of large estates and the division of the land,—it is always the same conflict which ends by producing a new one. The best policy of those in power would be so to moderate this conflict as to let it right itself without the destruction of either element. But this has not been granted to men, and it seems not to be the will of God.

220

A great work limits us for the moment, because we feel it above our powers; and only in so far as we afterwards incorporate it with our culture, and make it part of our mind and heart, does it become a dear and worthy object.

221

It is no wonder that we all more or less delight in the mediocre, because it leaves us in peace: it gives us the comfortable feeling of intercourse with what is like ourselves.

222

There is no use in reproving vulgarity, for it never changes.

223

We cannot escape a contradiction in ourselves; we must try to resolve it. If the contradiction comes from others, it does not affect us: it is their affair.

224

There are many things in the world that are at once good and excellent, but they do not come into contact.

225

Which is the best government? That which teaches us to govern ourselves.

226

When men have to do with women, they get spun off like a distaff.

227

It may well be that a man is at times horribly threshed by misfortunes, public and private: but the reckless flail of Fate, when it beats the rich sheaves, crushes only the straw; and the corn feels nothing of it and dances merrily on the floor, careless whether its way is to the mill or the furrow.

228

However probable it is that a desire may be fulfilled, there is always a doubt; and so when the desire is realised, it is always surprising.

Absurdities presented with good taste rouse disgust and admiration.

Of the best society it used to be said: their speech instructs the mind, and their silence the feelings.

Nothing is more terrible than ignorance in action.

Beauty and Genius must be kept afar if one would avoid becoming their slave.

We treat the aged with consideration, as we treat children.

An old man loses one of the greatest of human privileges: he is no more judged by his peers.

In the matter of knowledge, it has happened to me as to one who rises early, and in the dark impatiently awaits the dawn, and then the sun; but is blinded when it appears.

236

Great primeval powers, evolved in time or in eternity, work on unceasingly: whether to weal or to woe, is a matter of chance.

IV

237

People often say to themselves in life that they should avoid a
variety of occupation, and, more particularly, be the less willing to
enter upon new work the older they grow. But it is easy to talk,
easy to give advice to oneself and others. To grow old is itself to
enter upon a new business; all the circumstances change, and a man
must either cease acting altogether, or willingly and consciously
take over the new rôle.

238

Of the Absolute in the theoretical sense, I do not venture to speak;
but this I maintain: that if a man recognises it in its manifestation,
and always keeps his gaze fixed upon it, he will experience very
great reward.

239

To live in a great idea means to treat the impossible as though it
were possible. It is just the same with a strong character; and when
an idea and a character meet, things arise which fill the world with
wonder for thousands of years.

240

Napoleon lived wholly in a great idea, but he was unable to take
conscious hold of it. After utterly disavowing all ideals and denying
them any reality, he zealously strove to realise them. His clear,
incorruptible intellect could not, however, tolerate such a perpetual

conflict within; and there is much value in the thoughts which he was compelled, as it were, to utter, and which are expressed very peculiarly and with much charm.

241

He considered the idea as a thing of the mind, that had, it is true, no reality, but still, on passing away, left a residuum—a caput mortuum—to which some reality could not be altogether refused. We may think this a very perverse and material notion; but when he entertained his friends with the neverending consequences of his life and actions, in full belief and confidence in them, he expressed himself quite differently. Then, indeed, he was ready to admit that life produces life; that a fruitful act has effects to all time. He took pleasure in confessing that he had given a great impulse, a new direction, to the course of the world's affairs.

242

It always remains a very remarkable fact that men whose whole personality is almost all idea, are so extremely shy of all phantasy. In this case was Hamann, who could not bear the mention of "things of another world." He took occasion to express himself on this point in a certain paragraph, which he wrote in fourteen different ways; and still, apparently, he was never quite satisfied with it.

Two of these attempts have been preserved to us; a third we have ourselves attempted, which we are induced to print here by the preceding observations.

243

Man is placed as a real being in the midst of a real world, and endowed with such organs that he can perceive and produce the real and also the possible.

All healthy men have the conviction of their own existence and of an existence around them. However, even the brain contains a hollow spot, that is to say, a place in which no object is mirrored; just as in the eye itself there is a little spot that does not see. If a man pays particular attention to this spot and is absorbed in it, he falls into a state of mental sickness, has presentiments of "things of another world," which are, in reality, no things at all; possessing neither form nor limit, but alarming him like dark, empty tracts of night, and pursuing him as something more than phantoms, if he does not tear himself free from them.

244

To the several perversities of the day a man should always oppose only the great masses of universal history.

245

No one can live much with children without finding that they always react to any outward influence upon them.

246

With any specially childish nature the reaction is even passionate, while its action is energetic.

247

That is why children's lives are a series of refined judgments, not to say prejudices; and to efface a rapid but partial perception in order to make way for a more general one, time is necessary. To bear this in mind is one of the teacher's greatest duties.

248

Friendship can only be bred in practice and be maintained by practice. Affection, nay, love itself, is no help at all to friendship. True, active, productive friendship consists in keeping equal pace in life: in my friend approving my aims, while I approve his, and in thus moving forwards together steadfastly, however much our way of thought and life may vary.

V

249

In the world people take a man at his own estimate; but he must estimate himself at something. Disagreeableness is more easily tolerated than insignificance.

250

You can force anything on society so long as it has no sequel.

251

We do not learn to know men if they come to us; we must go to them to find out what they are.

252

That we have many criticisms to make on those who visit us, and that, as soon as they depart, we pass no very amiable judgment upon them, seems to me almost natural; for we have, so to speak, a right to measure them by our own standard. Even intelligent and fair-minded men hardly refrain from sharp censure on such occasions.

253

But if, on the contrary, we have been in their homes, and have seen them in their surroundings and habits and the circumstances which are necessary and inevitable for them; if we have seen the kind of influence they exert on those around them, or how they behave, it is only ignorance and ill-will that can find food for ridicule in what must appear to us in more than one sense worthy of respect.

254

What we call conduct and good manners obtains for us that which otherwise is to be obtained only by force, or not even by force.

255

Women's society is the element of good manners.

256

How can the character, the peculiar nature of a man, be compatible with good manners?

257

It is through his good manners that a man's peculiar nature should be made all the more conspicuous. Every one likes distinction, but it should not be disagreeable.

258

The most privileged position, in life as in society, is that of an educated soldier. Rough warriors, at any rate, remain true to their character, and as great strength is usually the cover for good nature, we get on with them at need.

259

No one is more troublesome than an awkward civilian. As his business is not with anything brutal or coarse, he might be expected to show delicacy of feeling.

260

When we live with people who have a delicate sense of what is fitting, we get quite anxious about them if anything happens to disturb this sense.

261

No one would come into a room with spectacles on his nose, if he knew that women at once lose any inclination to look at or talk to him.

262

A familiar in the place of a respectful demeanour is always ridiculous.

263

There is no outward sign of politeness that will be found to lack some deep moral foundation. The right kind of education would be that which conveyed the sign and the foundation at the same time.

264

A man's manners are the mirror in which he shows his portrait.

265

There is a politeness of the heart, and it is allied to love. It produces the most agreeable politeness of outward demeanour.

266

Voluntary dependence is the best state, and how should that be possible without love?

267

We are never further from our wishes than when we fancy we possess the object of them.

268

No one is more of a slave than he who thinks himself free without being so.

269

A man has only to declare himself free to feel at the same moment that he is limited. Should he venture to declare himself limited, he feels himself free.

270

Against the great superiority of another there is no remedy but love.

271

It is a terrible thing for an eminent man to be gloried in by fools.

272

It is said that no man is a hero to his valet. That is only because a hero can be recognised only by a hero. The valet will probably know how to appreciate his like,—his fellow-valet.

273

There is no greater consolation for mediocrity than that the genius is not immortal.

274

The greatest men are linked to their age by some weak point.

275

We generally take men to be more dangerous than they are.

276

Fools and wise folk are alike harmless. It is the half-wise, and the half-foolish, who are the most dangerous.

277

To see a difficult thing lightly handled gives us the impression of the impossible.

278

Difficulties increase the nearer we come to our aim.

279

Sowing is not so painful as reaping.

280

We are fond of looking to the future, because our secret wishes make us apt to turn in our favour the uncertainties which move about in it hither and thither.

281

It is not easy to be in any great assembly without thinking that the chance which brings so many people together will also make us meet our friends.

282

A man may live never so retired a life but he becomes a debtor or a creditor before he is aware of it.

283

If anyone meets us who owes us a debt of gratitude, it immediately crosses our mind. How often can we meet some one to whom we owe gratitude, without thinking of it!

284

To communicate oneself is Nature; to receive a communication as it is given is Culture.

285

No one would speak much in society if he were aware how often we misunderstand others.

286

It is only because we have not understood a thing that we cannot repeat it without alteration.

287

To make a long speech in the presence of others without flattering your audience, is to rouse dislike.

288

Every word that we utter rouses its contrary.

289

Contradiction and flattery make, both of them, bad conversation.

290

The pleasantest society is that in which there exists a genial deference amongst the members one towards another.

291

By nothing do men show their character more than by the things they laugh at.

292

The ridiculous springs from a moral contrast innocently presented to the senses.

293

The sensual man often laughs when there is nothing to laugh at. Whatever it is that moves him, he shows that he is pleased with himself.

294

An intelligent man finds almost everything ridiculous, a wise man hardly anything.

295

A man well on in years was reproved for still troubling himself about young women. 'It is the only means,' he replied, 'of regaining one's youth; and that is something every one wishes to do.'

296

A man does not mind being blamed for his faults, and being punished for them, and he patiently suffers much for the sake of them; but he becomes impatient if he is required to give them up.

297

Certain faults are necessary to the individual if he is to exist. We should not like old friends to give up certain peculiarities.

298

It is said of a man that he will soon die, when he acts in any way unlike himself.

299

What kind of faults in ourselves should we retain, nay, even cultivate? Those which rather flatter other people than offend them.

300

The passions are good or bad qualities, only intensified.

301

Our passions are, in truth, like the phoenix. When the old one burns away, the new one rises out of its ashes at once.

302

Great passions are hopeless diseases. That which could cure them is the first thing to make them really dangerous.

303

Passion is enhanced and tempered by avowal. In nothing, perhaps, is the middle course more desirable than in confidence and reticence towards those we love.

304

To sit in judgment on the departed is never likely to be equitable. We all suffer from life; who except God can call us to account? Let not their faults and sufferings, but what they have accomplished and done, occupy the survivors.

305

It is failings that show human nature, and merits that distinguish the individual; faults and misfortunes we all have in common; virtues belong to each one separately.

VI

306

The secret places in the way of life may not and cannot be revealed: there are rocks of offence on which every traveller must stumble. But the poet points to where they are.

307

It would not be worth while to see seventy years if all the wisdom of this world were foolishness with God.

308

The true is Godlike: we do not see it itself; we must guess at it through its manifestations.

309

The real scholar learns how to evolve the unknown from the known, and draws near the master.

310

In the smithy the iron is softened by blowing up the fire, and taking the dross from the bar. As soon as it is purified, it is beaten and pressed, and becomes firm again by the addition of fresh water. The same thing happens to a man at the hands of his teacher.

311

What belongs to a man, he cannot get rid of, even though he throws it away.

312

Of true religions there are only two: one of them recognises and worships the Holy that without form or shape dwells in and around us; and the other recognises and worships it in its fairest form. Everything that lies between these two is idolatry.

313

It is undeniable that in the Reformation the human mind tried to free itself; and the renaissance of Greek and Roman antiquity brought about the wish and longing for a freer, more seemly, and elegant life. The movement was favoured in no small degree by the fact that men's hearts aimed at returning to a certain simple state of nature, while the imagination sought to concentrate itself.

314

The Saints were all at once driven from heaven; and senses, thought, and heart were turned from a divine mother with a tender child, to the grown man doing good and suffering evil, who was later transfigured into a being half-divine in its nature, and then recognised and honoured as God himself. He stood against a background where the Creator had opened out the universe; a spiritual influence went out from him; his sufferings were adopted as an example, and his transfiguration was the pledge of everlastingness.

As a coal is revived by incense, so prayer revives the hopes of the heart.

From a strict point of view we must have a reformation of ourselves every day, and protest against others, even though it be in no religious sense.

It should be our earnest endeavour to use words coinciding as closely as possible with what we feel, see, think, experience, imagine, and reason. It is an endeavour which we cannot evade, and which is daily to be renewed.

Let every man examine himself, and he will find this a much harder task than he might suppose; for, unhappily, a man usually takes words as mere make-shifts; his knowledge and his thought are in most cases better than his method of expression.

False, irrelevant, and futile ideas may arise in ourselves and others, or find their way into us from without. Let us persist in the effort to remove them as far as we can, by plain and honest purpose.

As we grow older, the ordeals grow greater.

Where I cannot be moral, my power is gone.

320

A man is not deceived by others, he deceives himself.

321

Laws are all made by old people and by men. Youths and women want the exceptions, old people the rules.

322

It is not the intelligent man who rules, but intelligence; not the wise man, but wisdom.

323

To praise a man is to put oneself on his level.

324

It is not enough to know, we must also apply; it is not enough to will, we must also do.

325

Chinese, Indian, and Egyptian antiquities are never more than curiosities; it is well to make acquaintance with them; but in point of moral and æsthetic culture they can help us little.

The German runs no greater danger than to advance with and by the example of his neighbours. There is perhaps no nation that is fitter for the process of self-development; so that it has proved of the greatest advantage to Germany to have obtained the notice of the world so late.

Even men of insight do not see that they try to explain things which lie at the foundation of our experience, and in which we must simply acquiesce.

Yet still the attempt may have its advantage, as otherwise we should break off our researches too soon.

From this time forward, if a man does not apply himself to some art or handiwork, he will be in a bad way. In the rapid changes of the world, knowledge is no longer a furtherance; by the time a man has taken note of everything, he has lost himself.

Besides, in these days the world forces universal culture upon us, and so we need not trouble ourselves further about it; we must appropriate some particular culture.

The greatest difficulties lie where we do not look for them.

331

Our interest in public events is mostly the merest philistinism.

332

Nothing is more highly to be prized than the value of each day.

333

Pereant qui ante nos nostra dixerunt! This is so strange an utterance, that it could only have come from one who fancied himself autochthonous. The man who looks upon it as an honour to be descended from wise ancestors, will allow them at least as much common-sense as he allows himself.

334

Strictly speaking, everything depends upon a man's intentions; where these exist, thoughts appear; and as the intentions are, so are the thoughts.

335

If a man lives long in a high position, he does not, it is true, experience all that a man can experience; but he experiences things like them, and perhaps some things that have no parallel elsewhere.

VII

336

The first and last thing that is required of genius is love of truth.

337

To be and remain true to oneself and others, is to possess the noblest attribute of the greatest talents.

338

Great talents are the best means of conciliation.

339

The action of genius is in a way ubiquitous: towards general truths before experience, and towards particular truths after it.

340

An active scepticism is one which constantly aims at overcoming itself, and arriving by means of regulated experience at a kind of conditioned certainty.

341

The general nature of the sceptical mind is its tendency to inquire whether any particular predicate really attaches to any particular object; and the purpose of the inquiry is safely to apply in practice what has thus been discovered and proved.

342

The mind endowed with active powers and keeping with a practical object to the task that lies nearest, is the worthiest there is on earth.

343

Perfection is the measure of heaven, and the wish to be perfect the measure of man.

344

Not only what is born with him, but also what he acquires, makes the man.

345

A man is well equipped for all the real necessities of life if he trusts his senses, and so cultivates them that they remain worthy of being trusted.

346

The senses do not deceive; it is the judgment that deceives.

347

The lower animal is taught by its organs; man teaches his organs, and dominates them.

348

All direct invitation to live up to ideals is of doubtful value, particularly if addressed to women. Whatever the reason of it may be, a man of any importance collects round him a seraglio of a more or less religious, moral, and æsthetic character.

349

When a great idea enters the world as a Gospel, it becomes an offence to the multitude, which stagnates in pedantry; and to those who have much learning but little depth, it is folly.

350

Every idea appears at first as a strange visitor, and when it begins to be realised, it is hardly distinguishable from phantasy and phantastery.

351

This it is that has been called, in a good and in a bad sense, ideology; and this is why the ideologist is so repugnant to the hard-working, practical man of every day.

352

You may recognise the utility of an idea, and yet not quite understand how to make a perfect use of it.

353

Credo Deum! That is a fine, a worthy thing to say; but to recognise God where and as he reveals himself, is the only true bliss on earth.

354

Kepler said: 'My wish is that I may perceive the God whom I find everywhere in the external world, in like manner also within and inside me.' The good man was not aware that in that very moment the divine in him stood in the closest connection with the divine in the Universe.

355

What is predestination? It is this: God is mightier and wiser than we are, and so he does with us as he pleases.

356

Toleration should, strictly speaking, be only a passing mood; it ought to lead to acknowledgment and appreciation. To tolerate a person is to affront him.

357

Faith, Love, and Hope once felt, in a quiet sociable hour, a plastic impulse in their nature; they worked together and created a lovely image, a Pandora in the higher sense, Patience.

358

'I stumbled over the roots of the tree which I planted.' It must have been an old forester who said that.

359

A leaf blown by the wind often looks like a bird.

360

Does the sparrow know how the stork feels?

361

Lamps make oil-spots, and candles want snuffing; it is only the light of heaven that shines pure and leaves no stain.

362

If you miss the first button-hole, you will not succeed in buttoning up your coat.

363

A burnt child dreads the fire; an old man who has often been singed is afraid of warming himself.

It is not worth while to do anything for the world that we have with us, as the existing order may in a moment pass away. It is for the past and the future that we must work: for the past, to acknowledge its merits; for the future, to try to increase its value.

365

Let every man ask himself with which of his faculties he can and will somehow influence his age.

366

Let no one think that people have waited for him as for the Saviour.

367

Character in matters great and small consists in a man steadily pursuing the things of which he feels himself capable.

368

The man who wants to be active and has to be so, need only think of what is fitting at the moment, and he will make his way without difficulty. This is where women have the advantage, if they understand it.

369

The moment is a kind of public; a man must deceive it into believing that he is doing something; then it leaves us alone to go our way in secret; whereat its grandchildren cannot fail to be astonished.

There are men who put their knowledge in the place of insight.

In some states, as a consequence of the violent movements experienced in almost all directions, there has come about a certain overpressure in the system of education, the harm of which will be more generally felt hereafter; though even now it is perfectly well recognised by capable and honest authorities. Capable men live in a sort of despair over the fact that they are bound by the rules of their office to teach and communicate things which they look upon as useless and hurtful.

There is no sadder sight than the direct striving after the unconditioned in this thoroughly conditioned world.

Before the Revolution it was all effort; afterwards it all changed to demand.

Can a nation become ripe? That is a strange question. I would answer, Yes! if all the men could be born thirty years of age. But as youth will always be too forward and old age too backward, the really mature man is always hemmed in between them, and has to resort to strange devices to make his way through.

It does not look well for monarchs to speak through the press, for power should act and not talk. The projects of the liberal party always bear being read: the man who is overpowered may at least express his views in speech, because he cannot act. When Mazarin was shown some satirical songs on a new tax, 'Let them sing,' said he, 'as long as they pay.'

376

Vanity is a desire of personal glory, the wish to be appreciated, honoured, and run after, not because of one's personal qualities, merits, and achievements, but because of one's individual existence. At best, therefore, it is a frivolous beauty whom it befits.

377

The most important matters of feeling as of reason, of experience as of reflection, should be treated of only by word of mouth. The spoken word at once dies if it is not kept alive by some other word following on it and suited to the hearer. Observe what happens in social converse. If the word is not dead when it reaches the hearer, he murders it at once by a contradiction, a stipulation, a condition, a digression, an interruption, and all the thousand tricks of conversation. With the written word the case is still worse. No one cares to read anything to which he is not already to some extent accustomed: he demands the known and the familiar under an altered form. Still the written word has this advantage, that it lasts and can await the time when it is allowed to take effect.

378

Both what is reasonable and what is unreasonable have to undergo the like contradiction.

379

Dialectic is the culture of the spirit of contradiction, which is given to man that he may learn to perceive the differences between things.

380

With those who are really of like disposition with himself a man cannot long be at variance; he will always come to an agreement again. With those who are really of adverse disposition, he may in vain try to preserve harmony; he will always come to a separation again.

381

Opponents fancy they refute us when they repeat their own opinion and pay no attention to ours.

382

People who contradict and dispute should now and then remember that not every mode of speech is intelligible to every one.

383

Every man hears only what he understands.

384

I am quite prepared to find that many a reader will disagree with me; but when he has a thing before him in black and white, he must let it stand. Another reader may perhaps take up the very same copy and agree with me.

385

The truest liberality is appreciation.

386

For the strenuous man the difficulty is to recognise the merits of elder contemporaries and not let himself be hindered by their defects.

387

Some men think about the defects of their friends, and there is nothing to be gained by it. I have always paid attention to the merits of my enemies, and found it an advantage.

388

There are many men who fancy they understand whatever they experience.

389

The public must be treated like women: they must be told absolutely nothing but what they like to hear.

Every age of man has a certain philosophy answering to it. The child comes out as a realist: he finds himself as convinced that pears and apples exist as that he himself exists. The youth in a storm of inner passion is forced to turn his gaze within, and feel in advance what he is going to be: he is changed into an idealist. But the man has every reason to become a sceptic: he does well to doubt whether the means he has chosen to his end are the right ones. Before and during action he has every reason for keeping his understanding mobile, that he may not afterwards have to grieve over a false choice. Yet when he grows old he will always confess himself a mystic: he sees that so much seems to depend on chance; that folly succeeds and wisdom fails; that good and evil fortune are brought unexpectedly to the same level; so it is and so it has been, and old age acquiesces in that which is and was and will be.

391

When a man grows old he must consciously remain at a certain stage.

392

It does not become an old man to run after the fashion, either in thought or in dress. But he must know where he is, and what the others are aiming at.

What is called fashion is the tradition of the moment. All tradition carries with it a certain necessity for people to put themselves on a level with it.

393

We have long been busy with the critique of reason. I should like to see a critique of common-sense. It would be a real benefit to mankind if we could convincingly prove to the ordinary intelligence how far it can go; and that is just as much as it fully requires for life on this earth.

394

The thinker makes a great mistake when he asks after cause and effect: they both together make up the indivisible phenomenon.

395

All practical men try to bring the world under their hands; all thinkers, under their heads. How far each succeeds, they may both see for themselves.

396

Shall we say that a man thinks only when he cannot think out that of which he is thinking?

397

What is invention or discovery? It is the conclusion of what we were looking for.

398

It is with history as with nature and with everything of any depth, it may be past, present, or future: the further we seriously pursue it, the more difficult are the problems that appear. The man who is not afraid of them, but attacks them bravely, has a feeling of higher culture and greater ease the further he progresses.

399

Every phenomenon is within our reach if we treat it as an inclined plane, which is of easy ascent, though the thick end of the wedge may be steep and inaccessible.

400

If a man would enter upon some course of knowledge, he must either be deceived or deceive himself, unless external necessity irresistibly determines him. Who would become a physician if, at one and the same time, he saw before him all the horrible sights that await him?

401

How many years must a man do nothing before he can at all know what is to be done and how to do it!

402

Duty: where a man loves what he commands himself to do.

LITERATURE AND ART

403

When Madame Roland was on the scaffold, she asked for pen and paper, to note the peculiar thoughts that hovered about her on the last journey. It is a pity they were refused, for in a tranquil mind thoughts rise up at the close of life hitherto unthinkable; like blessed inward voices, alighting in glory on the summits of the past.

404

Literature is a fragment of fragments: the least of what happened and was spoken, has been written; and of the things that have been written, very few have been preserved.

405

And yet, with all the fragmentary nature of literature, we find thousand fold repetition; which shows how limited is man's mind and destiny.

406

Excellent work is unfathomable, approach it as you will.

407

It is not language in itself which is correct or forcible or elegant, but the mind that is embodied in it; and so it is not for a man to determine whether he will give his calculations or speeches or poems the desired qualities: the question is whether Nature has given him the intellectual and moral qualities which fit him for the work,—the intellectual power of observation and insight, the moral power of repelling the evil spirits that might hinder him from paying respect to truth.

408

The appeal to posterity springs from the pure, strong feeling of the existence of something imperishable; something that, even though it be not at once recognised, will in the end be gratified by finding the minority turn into a majority.

409

When a new literature succeeds, it obscures the effect of an earlier one, and its own effect predominates; so that it is well, from time to time, to look back. What is original in us is best preserved and quickened if we do not lose sight of those who have gone before us.

410

The most original authors of modern times are so, not because they produce what is new, but only because they are able to say things the like of which seem never to have been said before.

411

Thus the best sign of originality lies in taking up a subject and then developing it so fully as to make every one confess that he would hardly have found so much in it.

412

There are many thoughts that come only from general culture, like buds from green branches. When roses bloom, you see them blooming everywhere.

413

Lucidity is a due distribution of light and shade.' Hamann.

414

A man who has no acquaintance with foreign languages knows nothing of his own.

415

We must remember that there are many men who, without being productive, are anxious to say something important, and the results are most curious.

416

Deep and earnest thinkers are in a difficult position with regard to the public.

417

Some books seem to have been written, not to teach us anything, but to let us know that the author has known something.

418

An author can show no greater respect for his public than by never bringing it what it expects, but what he himself thinks right and proper in that stage of his own and others' culture in which for the time he finds himself.

419

The so-called Nature-poets are men of active talent, with a fresh stimulus and reaction from an over-cultured, stagnant, mannered epoch of art. They cannot avoid commonplace.

420

Productions are now possible which, without being bad, have no value. They have no value, because they contain nothing; and they are not bad, because a general form of good-workmanship is present to the author's mind.

421

All lyrical work must, as a whole, be perfectly intelligible, but in some particulars a little unintelligible.

422

A romance is a subjective epic in which the author begs leave to treat the world after his own ideas. The only question is, whether he has any ideas; the rest will follow of itself.

Subjective or so-called sentimental poetry has now been admitted to an equality with objective and descriptive. This was inevitable; because otherwise the whole of modern poetry would have to be discarded. It is now obvious that when men of truly poetical genius appear, they will describe more of the particular feelings of the inner life than of the general facts of the great life of the world. This has already taken place to such a degree that we have a poetry without figures of speech, which can by no means be refused all praise.

424

Superstition is the poetry of life, and so it does not hurt the poet to be superstitious.

425

That glorious hymn, Veni Creator Spiritus, is really an appeal to genius. That is why it speaks so powerfully to men of intellect and power.

426

Translators are like busy match-makers: they sing the praises of some half-veiled beauty, and extol her charms, and arouse an irresistible longing for the original.

427

A Spinoza in poetry becomes a Machiavelli in philosophy.

Against the three unities there is nothing to be said, if the subject is very simple; but there are times when thrice three unities, skilfully interwoven, produce a very pleasant effect.

429

The sentimentality of the English is humorous and tender; of the French, popular and pathetic; of the Germans, naïve and realistic.

430

Mysticism is the scholastic of the heart, the dialectic of the feelings.

431

If a man sets out to reproach an author with obscurity, he should first of all examine his own mind, to see if he is himself all clearness within. Twilight makes even plain writing illegible.

432

It is with books as with new acquaintances. At first we are highly delighted, if we find a general agreement,—if we are pleasantly moved on any of the chief sides of our existence. With a closer acquaintance differences come to light; and then reasonable conduct mainly consists in not shrinking back at once, as may happen in youth, but in keeping firm hold of the things in which we agree, and being quite clear about the things in which we differ, without on that account desiring any union.

433

In psychological reflection the greatest difficulty is this: that inner and outer must always be viewed in parallel lines, or, rather, interwoven. It is a continual systole and diastole, an inspiration and an expiration of the living soul. If this cannot be put into words, it should be carefully marked and noted.

434

My relations with Schiller rested on the decided tendency of both of us towards a single aim, and our common activity rested on the diversity of the means by which we endeavoured to attain that aim.

435

Once when a slight difference was mentioned between us, of which I was reminded by a passage in a letter of his, I made the following reflections: There is a great difference between a poet seeking the particular for the universal, and seeing the universal in the particular. The one gives rise to Allegory, where the particular serves only as instance or example of the general; but the other is the true nature of Poetry, namely, the expression of the particular without any thought of, or reference to, the general. If a man grasps the particular vividly, he also grasps the general, without being aware of it at the time; or he may make the discovery long afterwards.

436

There may be eclectic philosophers, but not an eclectic philosophy.

437

But every one is an eclectic who, out of the things that surround and take place about him, appropriates what is suited to his nature; and this is what is meant by culture and progress, in matters of theory or practice.

438

Various maxims of the ancients, which we are wont to repeat again and again, had a meaning quite different from that which is apt to attach to them in later times.

439

The saying that no one who is unacquainted with or a stranger to geometry should enter the philosopher's school, does not mean that a man must become a mathematician to attain the wisdom of the world.

440

Geometry is here taken in its primary elements, such as are contained in Euclid and laid before every beginner; and then it is the most perfect propædeutic and introduction to philosophy.

441

When a boy begins to understand that an invisible point must always come before a visible one, and that the shortest way between two points is a straight line, before he can draw it on his paper with a pencil, he experiences a certain pride and pleasure.

And he is not wrong; for he has the source of all thought opened to him; idea and reality, potentia et actu, are become clear; the philosopher has no new discovery to bring him; as a mathematician, he has found the basis of all thought for himself.

442

And if we turn to that significant utterance, Know thyself, we must not explain it in an ascetic sense. It is in nowise the self-knowledge of our modern hypochondrists, humorists, and self-tormentors. It simply means: pay some attention to yourself; take note of yourself; so that you may know how you come to stand towards those like you and towards the world. This involves no psychological torture; every capable man knows and feels what it means. It is a piece of good advice which every one will find of the greatest advantage in practice.

443

Let us remember how great the ancients were; and especially how the Socratic school holds up to us the source and standard of all life and action, and bids us not indulge in empty speculation, but live and do.

444

So long as our scholastic education takes us back to antiquity and furthers the study of the Greek and Latin languages, we may congratulate ourselves that these studies, so necessary for the higher culture, will never disappear.

445

If we set our gaze on antiquity and earnestly study it, in the desire to form ourselves thereon, we get the feeling as if it were only then that we really became men.

446

The pedagogue, in trying to write and speak Latin, has a higher and grander idea of himself than would be permissible in ordinary life.

447

In the presence of antiquity, the mind that is susceptible to poetry and art feels itself placed in the most pleasing ideal state of nature; and even to this day the Homeric hymns have the power of freeing us, at any rate, for moments, from the frightful burden which the tradition of several thousand years has rolled upon us.

448

There is no such thing as patriotic art and patriotic science. Both art and science belong, like all things great and good, to the whole world, and can be furthered only by a free and general interchange of ideas among contemporaries, with continual reference to the heritage of the past as it is known to us.

449

Poetical talent is given to peasant as well as to knight; all that is required is that each shall grasp his position and treat it worthily.

450

An historic sense means a sense so cultured that, in valuing the deserts and merits of its own time, it takes account also of the past.

451

The best that history gives us is the enthusiasm it arouses.

452

The historian's duty is twofold: first towards himself, then towards his readers. As regards himself, he must carefully examine into the things that could have happened; and, for the reader's sake, he must determine what actually did happen. His action towards himself is a matter between himself and his colleagues; but the public must not see into the secret that there is little in history which can be said to be positively determined.

453

The historian's duty is to separate the true from the false, the certain from the uncertain, and the doubtful from that which cannot be accepted.

454

It is seldom that any one of great age becomes historical to himself, and finds his contemporaries become historical to him, so that he neither cares nor is able to argue with any one.

On a closer examination of the matter, it will be found that the historian does not easily grasp history as something historical. In whatever age he may live, the historian always writes as though he himself had been present at the time of which he treats, instead of simply narrating the facts and movements of that time. Even the mere chronicler only points more or less to his own limitations, or the peculiarities of his town or monastery or age.

456

We really learn only from those books which we cannot criticise. The author of a book which we could criticise would have to learn from us.

457

That is the reason why the Bible will never lose its power; because, as long as the world lasts, no one can stand up and say: I grasp it as a whole and understand all the parts of it. But we say humbly: as a whole it is worthy of respect, and in all its parts it is applicable.

458

There is and will be much discussion as to the use and harm of circulating the Bible. One thing is clear to me: mischief will result, as heretofore, by using it phantastically as a system of dogma; benefit, as heretofore, by a loving acceptance of its teachings.

459

I am convinced that the Bible will always be more beautiful the more it is understood; the more, that is, we see and observe that every word which we take in a general sense and apply specially to ourselves, had, under certain circumstances of time and place, a peculiar, special, and directly individual reference.

460

The incurable evil of religious controversy is that while one party wants to connect the highest interest of humanity with fables and phrases, the other tries to rest it on things that satisfy no one.

461

If one has not read the newspapers for some months and then reads them all together, one sees, as one never saw before, how much time is wasted with this kind of literature.

462

The classical is health; and the romantic, disease.

463

Ovid remained classical even in exile: it is not in himself that he sees misfortune, but in his banishment from the metropolis of the world.

464

The romantic is already fallen into its own abysm. It is hard to imagine anything more degraded than the worst of the new productions.

Bodies which rot while they are still alive, and are edified by the detailed contemplation of their own decay; dead men who remain in the world for the ruin of others, and feed their death on the living,—to this have come our makers of literature.

When the same thing happened in antiquity, it was only as a strange token of some rare disease; but with the moderns the disease has become endemic and epidemic.

466

Literature decays only as men become more and more corrupt.

467

What a day it is when we must envy the men in their graves!

468

The things that are true, good, excellent, are simple and always alike, whatever their appearance may be. But the error that we blame is extremely manifold and varying; it is in conflict not only with the good and the true, but also with itself; it is self-contradictory. Thus it is that the words of blame in our literature must necessarily outnumber the words of praise.

469

The Greeks, whose poetry and rhetoric was of a simple and positive character, express approval more often than disapproval. With the

Latin writers it is the contrary; and the more poetry and the arts of speech decay, the more will blame swell and praise shrink.

470

'What are tragedies but the versified passions of people who make Heaven knows what out of the external world?'

471

There are certain empirical enthusiasts who are quite right in showing their enthusiasm over new productions that are good; but they are as ecstatic as if there were no other good work in the world at all.

472

In Sakontala the poet appears in his highest function. As the representative of the most natural condition of things, the finest mode of life, the purest moral endeavour, the worthiest majesty, and the most solemn worship, he ventures on common and ridiculous contrasts.

473

Shakespeare's Henry IV. If everything were lost that has ever been preserved to us of this kind of writing, the arts of poetry and rhetoric could be completely restored out of this one play.

Shakespeare's finest dramas are wanting here and there in facility: they are something more than they should be, and for that very reason indicate the great poet.

Shakespeare is dangerous reading for budding talents: he compels them to reproduce him, and they fancy they are producing themselves.

Yorick Sterne was the finest spirit that ever worked. To read him is to attain a fine feeling of freedom; his humour is inimitable, and it is not every kind of humour that frees the soul.

The peculiar value of so-called popular ballads is that their motives are drawn direct from nature. This, however, is an advantage of which the poet of culture could also avail himself, if he knew how to do it.

But in popular ballads there is always this advantage, that in the art of saying things shortly uneducated men are always better skilled than those who are in the strict sense of the word educated.

Gemüth = Heart. The translator must proceed until he reaches the untranslatable; and then only will he have an idea of the foreign nation and the foreign tongue.

480

When we say of a landscape that it has a romantic character, it is the secret feeling of the sublime taking the form of the past, or, what is the same thing, of solitude, absence, or seclusion.

481

The Beautiful is a manifestation of secret laws of nature, which, without its presence, would never have been revealed.

482

It is said: Artist, study nature! But it is no trifle to develop the noble out of the commonplace, or beauty out of uniformity.

483

When Nature begins to reveal her open secret to a man, he feels an irresistible longing for her worthiest interpreter, Art.

484

For all other Arts we must make some allowance; but to Greek Art alone we are always debtors.

485

There is no surer way of evading the world than by Art; and no surer way of uniting with it than by Art.

486

Even in the moments of highest happiness and deepest misery we need the Artist.

487

False tendencies of the senses are a kind of desire after realism, always better than that false tendency which expresses itself as idealistic longing.

488

The dignity of Art appears perhaps most conspicuously in Music; for in Music there is no material to be deducted. It is wholly form and intrinsic value, and it raises and ennobles all that it expresses.

489

It is only by Art, and especially by Poetry, that the imagination is regulated. Nothing is more frightful than imagination without taste.

490

If we were to despise Art on the ground that it is an imitation of Nature, it might be answered that Nature also imitates much else; further, that Art does not exactly imitate that which can be seen by the eyes, but goes back to that element of reason of which Nature consists and according to which Nature acts.

491

Further, the Arts also produce much out of themselves, and, on the other hand, add much where Nature fails in perfection, in that they possess beauty in themselves. So it was that Pheidias could sculpture a god although he had nothing that could be seen by the eye to imitate, but grasped the appearance which Zeus himself would have if he were to come before our eyes.

492

Art rests upon a kind of religious sense: it is deeply and ineradicably in earnest. Thus it is that Art so willingly goes hand in hand with Religion.

493

A noble philosopher spoke of architecture as frozen music; and it was inevitable that many people should shake their heads over his remark. We believe that no better repetition of this fine thought can be given than by calling architecture a speechless music.

494

Art is essentially noble; therefore the artist has nothing to fear from a low or common subject. Nay, by taking it up, he ennobles it; and so it is that we see the greatest artists boldly exercising their sovereign rights.

495

In every artist there is a germ of daring, without which no talent is conceivable.

496

All the artists who are already known to me from so many sides, I propose to consider exclusively from the ethical side; to explain from the subject-matter and method of their work the part played therein by time and place, nation and master, and their own indestructible personality; to mould them to what they became and to preserve them in what they were.

497

Art is a medium of what no tongue can utter; and thus it seems a piece of folly to try to convey its meaning afresh by means of words. But, by trying to do so, the understanding gains; and this, again, benefits the faculty in practice.

498

An artist who produces valuable work is not always able to give an account of his own or others' performances.

499

We know of no world except in relation to mankind; and we wish for no Art that does not bear the mark of this relation.

Higher aims are in themselves more valuable, even if unfulfilled, than lower ones quite attained.

Blunt naïvety, stubborn vigour, scrupulous observance of rule, and any other epithets which may apply to older German Art, are a part of every earlier and simpler artistic method. The older Venetians, Florentines, and others had it all too.

Because Albrecht Dürer, with his incomparable talent, could never rise to the idea of the symmetry of beauty, or even to the thought of a fitting conformity to the object in view, are we never to spurn the ground!

Albrecht Dürer had the advantage of a very profound realistic perception, an affectionate human sympathy with all present conditions. He was kept back by a gloomy phantasy, devoid both of form and foundation.

It would be interesting to show how Martin Schön stands near him, and how the merits of German Art were restricted to these two; and useful also to show that it was not evening every day.

505

In every Italian school the butterfly breaks loose from the chrysalis.

506

After Klopstock released us from rhyme, and Voss gave us models of prose, are we to make doggerel again like Hans Sachs?

507

Let us be many-sided! Turnips are good, but they are best mixed with chestnuts. And these two noble products of the earth grow far apart.

508

In every kind of Art there is a degree of excellence which may be reached, so to speak, by the mere use of one's own natural talents. But at the same time it is impossible to go beyond that point, unless Art comes to one's aid.

509

In the presence of Nature even moderate talent is always possessed of insight; hence drawings from Nature that are at all carefully done always give pleasure.

510

To make many sketches issue at last in a complete work is something that not even the best artists always achieve.

511

In the sphere of true Art there is no preparatory school, but there is a way of preparation; and the best preparation is the interest of the most insignificant pupil in the work of the master. Colour-grinders have often made excellent painters.

512

If an artist grasps Nature aright and contrives to give its form a nobler, freer grace, no one will understand the source of his inspiration, and every one will swear that he has taken it from the antique.

513

In studying the human form, let the painter reject what is exaggerated, false, and mechanical; but let him learn to grasp of what infinite grace the human body is capable.

514

Kant taught us the critique of the reason. We must have a critique of the senses if Art in general, and especially German Art, is ever to regain its tone and move forward on the path of life and happiness.

SCIENCE

515

In the sphere of natural science let us remember that we have always to deal with an insoluble problem. Let us prove keen and honest in attending to anything which is in any way brought to our notice, most of all when it does not fit in with our previous ideas. For it is only thereby that we perceive the problem, which does indeed lie in nature, but still more in man.

516

A man cannot well stand by himself, and so he is glad to join a party; because if he does not find rest there, he at any rate finds quiet and safety.

517

It is a misfortune to pass at once from observation to conclusion, and to regard both as of equal value; but it befalls many a student.

518

In the history of science and throughout the whole course of its progress we see certain epochs following one another more or less rapidly. Some important view is expressed, it may be original or only revived; sooner or later it receives recognition; fellow workers spring up; the outcome of it finds its way into the schools; it is taught and handed down; and we observe, unhappily, that it does not in the least matter whether the view be true or false. In either case its course is the same; in either case it comes in the end to be a mere phrase, a lifeless word stamped on the memory.

519

First let a man teach himself, and then he will be taught by others.

520

Theories are usually the over-hasty efforts of an impatient understanding that would gladly be rid of phenomena, and so puts in their place pictures, notions, nay, often mere words. We may surmise, or even see quite well, that such theories are make-shifts; but do not passion and party-spirit love a make-shift at all times? And rightly, too, because they stand in so much need of it.

521

It is difficult to know how to treat the errors of the age. If a man oppose them, he stands alone; if he surrender to them, they bring him neither joy nor credit.

522

There are some hundred Christian sects, every one of them acknowledging God and the Lord in its own way, without troubling themselves further about one another. In the study of nature, nay, in every study, things must of necessity come to the same pass. For what is the meaning of every one speaking of toleration, and trying to prevent others from thinking and expressing themselves after their own fashion?

523

To communicate knowledge by means of analogy appears to me a process equally useful and pleasant. The analogous case is not there to force itself on the attention or prove anything; it offers a comparison with some other case, but is not in union with it. Several analogous cases do not join to form a seried row: they are like good society, which always suggests more than it grants.

524

To err is to be as though truth did not exist. To lay bare the error to oneself and others is retrospective discovery.

525

With the growth of knowledge our ideas must from time to time be organised afresh. The change takes place usually in accordance with new maxims as they arise, but it always remains provisional.

526

When we find facts within our knowledge exhibited by some new method, or even, it may be, described in a foreign language, they receive a peculiar charm of novelty and wear a fresh air.

527

If two masters of the same art differ in their statement of it, in all likelihood the insoluble problem lies midway between them.

528

The orbits of certainties touch one another; but in the interstices there is room enough for error to go forth and prevail.

529

We more readily confess to errors, mistakes, and shortcomings in our conduct than in our thought.

530

And the reason of it is that the conscience is humble and even takes a pleasure in being ashamed. But the intellect is proud, and if forced to recant is driven to despair.

531

This also explains how it is that truths which have been recognised are at first tacitly admitted, and then gradually spread, so that the very thing which was obstinately denied appears at last as something quite natural.

532

Ignorant people raise questions which were answered by the wise thousands of years ago.

533

When a man sees a phenomenon before him, his thoughts often range beyond it; when he hears it only talked about, he has no thoughts at all.

534

Authority. Man cannot exist without it, and yet it brings in its train just as much of error as of truth. It perpetuates one by one things which should pass away one by one; it rejects that which should be preserved and allows it to pass away; and it is chiefly to blame for mankind's want of progress.

535

Authority—the fact, namely, that something has already happened or been said or decided, is of great value; but it is only a pedant who demands authority for everything.

536

An old foundation is worthy of all respect, but it must not take from us the right to build afresh wherever we will.

537

Our advice is that every man should remain in the path he has struck out for himself, and refuse to be overawed by authority, hampered by prevalent opinion, or carried away by fashion.

538

The various branches of knowledge always tend as a whole to stray away from life, and return thither only by a roundabout way.

539

For they are, in truth, text-books of life: they gather outer and inner experiences into a general and connected whole.

540

An important fact, an ingenious aperçu, occupies a very great number of men, at first only to make acquaintance with it; then to understand it; and afterwards to work it out and carry it further.

541

On the appearance of anything new the mass of people ask: What is the use of it? And they are not wrong. For it is only through the use of anything that they can perceive its value.

542

The truly wise ask what the thing is in itself and in relation to other things, and do not trouble themselves about the use of it, — in other words, about the way in which it may be applied to the necessities of existence and what is already known. This will soon be discovered by minds of a very different order—minds that feel the joy of living, and are keen, adroit, and practical.

543

Every investigator must before all things look upon himself as one who is summoned to serve on a jury. He has only to consider how far the statement of the case is complete and clearly set forth by the evidence. Then he draws his conclusion and gives his vote, whether it be that his opinion coincides with that of the foreman or not.

544

And in acting thus he remains equally at ease whether the majority agree with him or he finds himself in a minority. For he has done what he could: he has expressed his convictions; and he is not master of the minds or hearts of others.

545

In the world of science, however, these sentiments have never been of much account. There everything depends on making opinion prevail and dominate; few men are really independent; the majority draws the individual after it.

546

The history of philosophy, of science, of religion, all shows that opinions spread in masses, but that that always comes to the front which is more easily grasped, that is to say, is most suited and agreeable to the human mind in its ordinary condition. Nay, he who has practised self-culture in the higher sense may always reckon upon meeting an adverse majority.

547

There is much that is true which does not admit of being calculated; just as there are a great many things that cannot be brought to the test of a decisive experiment.

548

It is just for this that man stands so high, that what could not otherwise be brought to light should be brought to light in him.

What is a musical string, and all its mechanical division, in comparison with the musician's ear? May we not also say, what are the elementary phenomena of nature itself compared with man, who must control and modify them all before he can in any way assimilate them to himself?

549

To a new truth there is nothing more hurtful than an old error.

550

The ultimate origin of things is completely beyond our faculties; hence when we see anything come into being, we look upon it as having been already there. This is why we find the theory of emboîtement intelligible.

551

There are many problems in natural science on which we cannot fittingly speak unless we call metaphysics to our aid; but not the wisdom of the schools, which consists in mere verbiage. It is that which was before physics, exists with it, and will be after it.

552

Since men are really interested in nothing but their own opinions, every one who puts forward an opinion looks about him right and left for means of strengthening himself and others in it. A man avails himself of the truth so long as it is serviceable; but he seizes on what is false with a passionate eloquence as soon as he can make a momentary use of it; whether it be to dazzle others with it as a kind of half-truth, or to employ it as a stopgap for effecting an apparent union between things that have been disjointed. This experience at first caused me annoyance, and then sorrow; and now it is a source of mischievous satisfaction. I have pledged myself never again to expose a proceeding of this kind.

553

Everything that we call Invention or Discovery in the higher sense of the word is the serious exercise and activity of an original feeling for truth, which, after a long course of silent cultivation, suddenly flashes out into fruitful knowledge. It is a revelation working from within on the outer world, and lets a man feel that he is made in the image of God. It is a synthesis of World and Mind, giving the most blessed assurance of the eternal harmony of things.

554

A man must cling to the belief that the incomprehensible is comprehensible; otherwise he would not try to fathom it.

555

There are pedants who are also rascals, and they are the worst of all.

556

A man does not need to have seen or experienced everything himself. But if he is to commit himself to another's experiences and his way of putting them, let him consider that he has to do with three things—the object in question and two subjects.

557

The supreme achievement would be to see that stating a fact is starting a theory.

558

If I acquiesce at last in some ultimate fact of nature, it is, no doubt, only resignation; but it makes a great difference whether the resignation takes place at the limits of human faculty, or within the hypothetical boundaries of my own narrow individuality.

559

If we look at the problems raised by Aristotle, we are astonished at his gift of observation. What wonderful eyes the Greeks had for many things! Only they committed the mistake of being over-hasty, of passing straightway from the phenomenon to the explanation of it, and thereby produced certain theories that are quite inadequate. But this is the mistake of all times, and still made in our own day.

560

Hypotheses are cradle-songs by which the teacher lulls his scholars to sleep. The thoughtful and honest observer is always learning more and more of his limitations; he sees that the further knowledge spreads, the more numerous are the problems that make their appearance.

561

Our mistake is that we doubt what is certain and want to establish what is uncertain. My maxim in the study of Nature is this: hold fast what is certain and keep a watch on what is uncertain.

562

What a master a man would be in his own subject if he taught nothing useless!

563

The greatest piece of folly is that every man thinks himself compelled to hand down what people think they have known.

564

If many a man did not feel obliged to repeat what is untrue, because he has said it once, the world would have been quite different.

565

Every man looks at the world lying ready before him, ordered and fashioned into a complete whole, as after all but an element out of which his endeavour is to create a special world suited to himself. Capable men lay hold of the world without hesitation and try to shape their course as best they can; others dally over it, and some doubt even of their own existence.

The man who felt the full force of this fundamental truth would dispute with no one, but look upon another's mode of thought equally with his own, as merely a phenomenon. For we find almost daily that one man can think with ease what another cannot possibly think at all; and that, too, not in matters which might have some sort of effect upon their common weal or woe, but in things which cannot touch them at all.

566

There is nothing more odious than the majority; it consists of a few powerful men to lead the way; of accommodating rascals and submissive weaklings; and of a mass of men who trot after them, without in the least knowing their own mind.

567

When I observe the luminous progress and expansion of natural science in modern times, I seem to myself like a traveller going eastwards at dawn, and gazing at the growing light with joy, but also with impatience; looking forward with longing to the advent of the full and final light, but, nevertheless, having to turn away his eyes when the sun appeared, unable to bear the splendour he had awaited with so much desire.

568

We praise the eighteenth century for concerning itself chiefly with analysis. The task remaining to the nineteenth is to discover the false syntheses which prevail, and to analyse their contents anew.

569

A school may be regarded as a single individual who talks to himself for a hundred years, and takes an extraordinary pleasure in his own being, however foolish and silly it may be.

570

In science it is a service of the highest merit to seek out those fragmentary truths attained by the ancients, and to develop them further.

571

If a man devotes himself to the promotion of science, he is firstly opposed, and then he is informed that his ground is already occupied. At first men will allow no value to what we tell them, and then they behave as if they knew it all themselves.

572

Nature fills all space with her limitless productivity. If we observe merely our own earth, everything that we call evil and unfortunate is so because Nature cannot provide room for everything that comes into existence, and still less endow it with permanence.

573

Everything that comes into being seeks room for itself and desires duration: hence it drives something else from its place and shortens its duration.

574

There is so much of cryptogamy in phanerogamy that centuries will not decipher it.

575

What a true saying it is that he who wants to deceive mankind must before all things make absurdity plausible.

576

The further knowledge advances, the nearer we come to the unfathomable: the more we know how to use our knowledge, the better we see that the unfathomable is of no practical use.

577

The finest achievement for a man of thought is to have fathomed what may be fathomed, and quietly to revere the unfathomable.

578

The discerning man who acknowledges his limitations is not far off perfection.

579

There are two things of which a man cannot be careful enough: of obstinacy if he confines himself to his own line of thought; of incompetency, if he goes beyond it.

580

Incompetency is a greater obstacle to perfection than one would think.

581

The century advances; but every individual begins anew.

582

What friends do with us and for us is a real part of our life; for it strengthens and advances our personality. The assault of our enemies is not part of our life; it is only part of our experience; we throw it off and guard ourselves against it as against frost, storm, rain, hail, or any other of the external evils which may be expected to happen.

583

A man cannot live with every one, and therefore he cannot live for every one. To see this truth aright is to place a high value upon one's friends, and not to hate or persecute one's enemies. Nay, there is hardly any greater advantage for a man to gain than to find out, if he can, the merits of his opponents: it gives him a decided ascendency over them.

584

Every one knows how to value what he has attained in life; most of all the man who thinks and reflects in his old age. He has a comfortable feeling that it is something of which no one can rob him.

585

The best metempsychosis is for us to appear again in others.

586

It is very seldom that we satisfy ourselves; all the more consoling is it to have satisfied others.

587

We look back upon our life only as on a thing of broken pieces, because our misses and failures are always the first to strike us, and outweigh in our imagination what we have done, and attained.

588

The sympathetic youth sees nothing of this; he reads, enjoys, and uses the youth of one who has gone before him, and rejoices in it with all his heart, as though he had once been what he now is.

589

Science helps us before all things in this, that it somewhat lightens the feeling of wonder with which Nature fills us; then, however, as life becomes more and more complex, it creates new facilities for the avoidance of what would do us harm and the promotion of what will do us good.

590

It is always our eyes alone, our way of looking at things. Nature alone knows what she means now, and what she had meant in the past.

NATURE: APHORISMS

Nature! We are surrounded by her and locked in her clasp: powerless to leave her, and powerless to come closer to her. Unasked and unwarned she takes us up into the whirl of her dance, and hurries on with us till we are weary and fall from her arms.

She creates new forms without end: what exists now, never was before; what was, comes not again; all is new and yet always the old.

We live in the midst of her and are strangers. She speaks to us unceasingly and betrays not her secret. We are always influencing her and yet can do her no violence.

Individuality seems to be all her aim, and she cares nought for individuals. She is always building and always destroying, and her workshop is not to be approached.

Nature lives in her children only, and the mother, where is she? She is the sole artist,—out of the simplest materials the greatest diversity; attaining, with no trace of effort, the finest perfection, the closest precision, always softly veiled. Each of her works has an essence of its own; every shape that she takes is in idea utterly isolated; and yet all forms one.

She plays a drama; whether she sees it herself, we know not; and yet she plays it for us, who stand but a little way off.

There is constant life in her, motion and development; and yet she remains where she was. She is eternally changing, nor for a moment does she stand still. Of rest she knows nothing, and to all stagnation she has affixed her curse. She is steadfast; her step is measured, her exceptions rare, her laws immutable.

She has thought, and she ponders unceasingly; not as a man, but as Nature. The meaning of the whole she keeps to herself, and no one can learn it of her.

Men are all in her, and she in all men. With all she plays a friendly game, and rejoices the more a man wins from her. With many her game is so secret, that she brings it to an end before they are aware of it.

Even what is most unnatural is Nature; even the coarsest Philistinism has something of her genius. Who does not see her everywhere, sees her nowhere aright.

She loves herself, and clings eternally to herself with eyes and hearts innumerable. She has divided herself that she may be her own delight. She is ever making new creatures spring up to delight in her, and imparts herself insatiably.

She rejoices in illusion. If a man destroys this in himself and others, she punishes him like the hardest tyrant. If he follows her in confidence, she presses him to her heart as it were her child.

Her children are numberless. To no one of them is she altogether niggardly; but she has her favourites, on whom she lavishes much, and for whom she makes many a sacrifice. Over the great she has spread the shield of her protection.

She spurts forth her creatures out of nothing, and tells them not whence they come and whither they go. They have only to go their way: she knows the path.

Her springs of action are few, but they never wear out: they are always working, always manifold.

The drama she plays is always new, because she is always bringing new spectators. Life is her fairest invention, and Death is her device for having life in abundance.

She envelops man in darkness, and urges him constantly to the light. She makes him dependent on the earth, heavy and sluggish, and always rouses him up afresh.

She creates wants, because she loves movement. How marvellous that she gains it all so easily! Every want is a benefit, soon satisfied, soon growing again. If she gives more, it is a new source of desire; but the balance quickly rights itself.

Every moment she starts on the longest journeys, and every moment reaches her goal.

She amuses herself with a vain show; but to us her play is all-important.

She lets every child work at her, every fool judge of her, and thousands pass her by and see nothing; and she has her joy in them all, and in them all finds her account.

Man obeys her laws even in opposing them: he works with her even when he wants to work against her.

Everything she gives is found to be good, for first of all she makes it indispensable. She lingers, that we may long for presence; she hurries by, that we may not grow weary of her.

Speech or language she has none; but she creates tongues and hearts through which she feels and speaks.

Her crown is Love. Only through Love can we come near her. She puts gulfs between all things, and all things strive to be interfused. She isolates everything, that she may draw everything together. With a few draughts from the cup of Love she repays for a life full of trouble.

She is all things. She rewards herself and punishes herself; and in herself rejoices and is distressed. She is rough and gentle, loving and terrible, powerless and almighty. In her everything is always present. Past or Future she knows not. The Present is her Eternity. She is kind. I praise her with all her works. She is wise and still. No one can force her to explain herself, or frighten her into a gift that she does not give willingly. She is crafty, but for a good end; and it is best not to notice her cunning.

She is whole and yet never finished. As she works now, so can she work for ever.

To every one she appears in a form of his own. She hides herself in a thousand names and terms, and is always the same.

She has placed me in this world; she will also lead me out of it. I trust myself to her. She may do with me as she pleases. She will not hate her work. I did not speak of her. No! what is true and what is false, she has spoken it all. Everything is her fault, everything is her merit.

THE END

www.ingramcontent.com/pod-product-compliance
Lightning Source LLC
Chambersburg PA
CBHW011507170626
46812CB00008B/3000